RA

"Shut up and get t

McBean started laughing and Slocum felt a heavy blow to the side of his head. He rolled away, seeing Schmidt coming after him. Kicking the Smith & Wesson from his hand, he tumbled over closer to the edge of the cave. He looked up into the barrel of McBean's Winchester and just managed to push out of the cave, down into the thundering water as McBean's rifle discharged . . .

DON'T MISS THESE
ALL-ACTION WESTERN SERIES
FROM THE BERKLEY PUBLISHING GROUP

THE GUNSMITH by J. R. Roberts
> Clint Adams was a legend among lawmen, outlaws, and ladies. They called him . . . the Gunsmith.

LONGARM by Tabor Evans
> The popular long-running series about U.S. Deputy Marshal Long—his life, his loves, his fight for justice.

LONE STAR by Wesley Ellis
> The blazing adventures of Jessica Starbuck and the martial arts master Ki. Over eight million copies in print.

SLOCUM by Jake Logan
> Today's longest-running action Western. John Slocum rides a deadly trail of hot blood and cold steel.

JAKE LOGAN

SLOCUM AND THE SNAKE GULCH SWINDLERS

BERKLEY BOOKS, NEW YORK

SLOCUM AND THE SNAKE GULCH SWINDLERS

A Berkley Book / published by arrangement with
the author

PRINTING HISTORY
Berkley edition / February 1995

ISBN: 0-425-14570-0

BERKLEY®
Berkley Books are published by The Berkley Publishing Group,
200 Madison Avenue, New York, New York 10016.
BERKLEY and the "B" design
are trademarks belonging to Berkley Publishing Corporation.

PRINTED IN THE UNITED STATES OF AMERICA

10 9 8 7 6 5 4 3 2 1

Thanks go to
Eric Kuby, an inspiring
childhood pal, and
Gary Goldstein, without whom
there would be no dedication page

SLOCUM AND THE
SNAKE GULCH SWINDLERS

1

John Slocum saw that his chance was at hand, that fortune, in the guise of Gary Clarkson, was smiling down upon him. He'd just gotten to Lewiston, in Idaho Territory, stabled his exhausted horse, and sauntered over to a saloon when he was tapped by his old buddy for a job. The money was good. Good enough to get Slocum thinking on his dream of raising horses. Every man has a dream he holds above all else. Slocum always had had a hankering to buy up enough ponies to start a little horse ranch in the Wind River Mountains.

And nearby, at the juncture of the Weiser, Payette, and Boise rivers, were the finest horses in the country. The Nez Percé used to trade there. Slocum had once bought some ponies from Old Chief Joseph, and had found the tribe to be friendly. The old chief was dead and times had turned sour for the Indians, but Slocum made up his mind to pay the tribe a visit as soon as he got his reward.

The mission was simple, to return a gold mine deed to some rich fool who'd trusted his foreman too well. Clarkson, a marshal now, said all his men were busy, it being Saturday night, so he could reasonably hand the job to Slocum, if he left right away. A fresh horse was provided and Slocum saddled her up.

He rode till morning, following the wagon trails through the valleys and a scrappy, half-laid supply road, and then up, up into the hilly wilderness. Although the route had been passable and no rattlesnakes or other pests had troubled him, the blue-roan had been acting up since the first mile outside Lewiston. It made Slocum wonder how far he should trust the judgment of the marshal, who'd recommended the animal.

Easy money was never as sweet as it sounded, he thought, sniffing something foul-smelling in the wind.

Someone cleared her throat from behind the pine scrub. Slocum drew the reins to one side to stop and listen.

"The end is near. Cook her with camas, sisters. The good blue and the white that kills."

The black-haired roan rebelled at the hoarse words, rearing up and launching into a series of prancing back kicks. By the time Slocum regained control, the speaker of them had vanished. To be fair, he couldn't entirely blame the roan. She was too easily spooked, it was true, but Slocum was getting the creeps, as well. The closer he'd come to Snake Gulch, the heavier the sense of foreboding, the more acrid the air had grown. Perhaps it was the sulfur used in these mining camps.

As the fog dissipated now, Slocum saw up ahead a clearing and beyond it a squat cottage of rough logs. He prodded the roan onward.

A boy peered from the window of the log house, Slocum noticed, as he neared the cabin, continuing along the trail. The boy listened to a woman's high, thin voice reciting from the Bible.

"They heard I was groaning, with no one to comfort me. All my enemies heard of my trouble; they are glad that You have done it. Bring on the day You have announced, and let them be as I am."

The boy at the window darted out of the cabin, running to just beyond arm's reach of Slocum. He smiled, but stammered, too timid to say whatever he had in mind.

Slocum casually took off his Stetson and scratched the side of his head, keeping an eye on the boy. He looked like an okay kid, perhaps a bit too hopeful for his own good. His big blue eyes were a little too trusting. It was like he was asking for trouble, but Slocum set aside his concern. He was growing too cynical, he told himself. An innocent child had every right to be easy with his trust. He'd learn about the world in due time.

"Howdy, son," Slocum said genially. "Didn't reckon on civilized family folk like you making a stand on this rocky bit of wilderness. Tell me, friend, this place got a name?"

The boy nodded, still a bit bashful.

Slocum was ready to move on. He hadn't slept a full night of the past four, and it was quickly catching up to him. He gave the boy a wink. "Town's got a name," he said. "Bet it's a devilish sort of name, like Snake Gulch. Tell me if that ain't the truth."

The boy nodded again. He could tell this man was no miner, that he'd come to town for a special reason. Maybe he had news from his mother. His father had sure had a bad time this winter without her. When she came back, he knew, everything would be all right again. "You come from Lewiston, ain't you?" the boy asked.

"Yep, but I wasn't there an hour if that."

The boy shrugged off his disappointment. "D'you see them old, old Injun sisters just now? They was here right before you came."

Slocum shook his head. "Can't say I did." But he thought of that strange whispering that had spooked his roan.

"They plucked this moltin' bird from out that there tree. It was a sign, I reckon. I saw 'em just before from Widder Parkens' window, the three Injuns by the red fir yonder. I saw 'em twist the bird's little neck and then I blinked and they was gone."

"Well, don't think on it too hard," Slocum said. "I best be heading on. Nice meeting you, son." He tipped his hat and was about to ride on, when he heard the widow's voice rising from inside the cabin.

"Let tears stream down like a torrent day and night!" she read. "Give yourself no rest, your eyes no respite!"

Slocum smiled with recognition. "Lamentations," he remarked. "Got to know that by heart back in the war." Then a sour thought occurred to him. It was Sunday.

Slocum motioned the boy over closer. "Listen, son, I'm sorry to be interrupting your religious lessons. In fact, I believe you best get back inside. But before you go, kindly tell me if there's a saloon open on the Lord's day up here in Snake Gulch."

"Matter of fact," the boy said, puffing up his chest, "my paw's got the best dang saloon in all of Snake Gulch. He calls it Banjo's Saloon, 'cause that's his Christian name, and it's just up the way over yonder."

Slocum almost said "Amen." He thanked the boy and told him to get back to his Bible class.

But the boy stood his ground. "Oh, I'll lead you up the way," he said. "Evan Baines's my name."

"John Slocum," he said. "Mighty glad to know you, and thanks for offering, son, but I can find it on my own." The boy looked hurt, so Slocum relented, dismounting from the black roan and patting the boy on the shoulder as they strolled along.

Evan's eyes widened as he spotted the ebony handle of the stranger's Colt peaking from his holster.

"You won't get into any trouble now, dodging Bible class?"

"Naw. The Widder Parkens don't notice nothing once she gets started on Lamentations." Evan spoke rapidly, his words cascading over one another, anxious lest he get sent back. Truth be told, he was convinced Lydia Parkens was an evil witch who'd singled him out in particular to torment. Every Sunday she cast a spell, sending all the other children to slow-breathing slumbers, leaving Evan alone, intimidated, and alert.

"She reads Lamentations near all the time, just like it's a spell," Evan confided. "Nothing's gone right for her since Miss Angelica, her sister, come to the Gulch. Mr. Parkens, the widder's husband before she was a widder, he tried to talk Miss Angelica into becoming a respectable lady again, after she'd turned into a whore."

"Personally, Evan Baines," Slocum said and cut the boy off with a laugh, "I'd rather hear a woman's story from her own lips, if and when she feels the need of telling it. Otherwise, I find it's always wiser not to look too closely into a woman's dealings. How old are you, Evan?"

"Be fourteen come summer," Evan said, again puffing up his narrow chest. The boy's slight build made him look younger than his years.

He had led Slocum out of the gently upward sloping forest on the outskirts of Snake Gulch, past a dozen or so cottages made of rough logs. The path leveled off on a plateau and widened into an avenue of mud, flanked by single-story frame buildings and the rarer two-story shops with porches and balconies. Beyond the plateau, in the distance, loomed a denuded hill, surrounded by miners' shanties.

"Here's my paw's place," the boy said with evident pride. It was one of the older buildings on the street, a sprawling pine-plank affair, rundown and buckling, though probably no more than three years old.

"Generally speaking," Slocum said to Evan, "I'd stable this animal myself before doing anything further. But I have a mighty thirst and the roan and I ain't the best of friends. Course, even an inferior horse deserves being looked after right."

Slocum and the roan eyed each other with distaste. "This here is the orneriest beast I ever met," Slocum continued. "You'd think she'd made her mind up to avoid Snake Gulch at all costs. Every chance she had, she tried to go the other way. Got to the point I knew which way to go simply by countermanding her." Slocum patted the horse's flank and grinned back at Evan.

The boy liked to listen to the worldly stranger and hoped suddenly that he'd come to settle down. "Why you aimin' to come here, anyways?" he asked.

"Reckon I was told there was a young feller in these parts who could use a Blackfoot tomahawk from the Baker Massacre." Slocum pulled the battle axe from his saddlebag and handed it to Evan.

"For me?" Evan asked, awestruck.

"It's yours if you'll see this horse gets some oats and water."

"Ain't no problem taking her to the stable. Nobody'd expect you to give me anything but maybe a nickel for that."

"I like an honest lad. That's a friend." Slocum flipped him a nickel. The boy held out the axe.

"Keep it, son. Never know when it might come in handy." Slocum slung the saddlebags over his shoulder and turned the reins over to Evan. "Don't let me get you in trouble," he added. "Might be a good idea to check in with that widow afterwards. Reckon she must be near finished with Lamentations."

As Slocum watched Evan lead the roan around the corner, he tried to get a sense of the sleepy town, now stirring to life. Down the street a man cracked his whip and got his wagon rolling. Around the side street Evan had gone down came the ringing of a blacksmith's anvil.

Slocum pushed through the batwings of the saloon and entered a dusty room filled with rough-hewn tables and stools. He could make out three men sitting in conversation at the far corner of a long bar. One moved in back of the bar upon seeing Slocum.

"Howdy," Slocum said, recognizing Evan's features in the bartender's face, especially the deep blue eyes. Banjo Baines was a midgety, red-cheeked man, perhaps a former bare-knuckle fighter now way past his prime, but not without some fight left in his arm. The extra pounds on his already stocky build and the black toupee that kept slipping to one side in the drafty saloon indicated it had been considerable time since he'd received any female attentions.

"What'll it be? Whiskey, eh?" Baines said, sizing him up. Slocum nodded and took some silver from his pocket.

"Morning's morning. First one's on the house." Banjo poured out a shot of a local version of whiskey and then walked back to the end of the bar, pouring another round for a large bearded man in a red woollen shirt and a smaller man with a handlebar mustache.

As Slocum's eyes adjusted to the dim light, he saw that past the three men the saloon opened into a side room for dancing. A staircase led to a gallery overlooking that room, and there were several doors beyond the gallery's railing.

"What you squintin' at?" the mustachioed man yelled down the bar to Slocum. "Want me to draw a map of the dump for you? The exit's that way."

Banjo grabbed hold of the man's elbow. "Blacky," he said, "I ain't gonna have you startin' up today like you finished off last night. Clear out now, if you ain't got the decency to hold your tongue in line before lunchtime."

Blacky grabbed Banjo's face between his hands. "Pucker up, darlin'. When you talk like that you sound just like that old whore, Flo . . . and it drives me wild as a toad in heat."

The bearded man laughed heartily at that.

"Er, now, McBean. Don't you go encouraging Blacky. He surely don't need no encouragin'."

Blacky continued to press the barman's face. "It ain't McBean, it's you that's encouragin' me, darlin'."

The bearded man called McBean laughed even harder.

Slocum called over to Blacky. "If you have a quarrel to pick with me, Blacky, I'd appreciate if you'd get to it and stop wasting time making love to the barkeep."

Blacky let go of Banjo's face and held his arms out to the sides and poised above his gunbelt as he slowly turned to face Slocum. "Say your prayers, stranger," Blacky snarled. But before he managed to touch his revolver, Slocum pitched his shot glass at the man's temple. As though hit by a lightning bolt, Blacky crumpled to his knees.

McBean stepped over to Blacky and set him back on his feet with a single tug. Then he marched him to the saloon doors, saying loudly, "Get lost, you drunken buzzard."

Blacky rubbed the bump emerging from his forehead, snarled again, and made as if to have another go for Slocum, but McBean said something in his ear and shoved him out into the street.

McBean laughed as he walked back over to the bar. "You're pretty swift with the glassware, stranger," he said to Slocum. "That Blacky sure does have all the luck. Why, if he'd tried that on anyone besides you, he'd've been laid out next to these geese." He pointed to a pair of large gray-brown geese with white chin straps, lying in a pool of blood on a nearby table.

"That would've been no fun for me," Slocum replied. "Generally it's not so easy for a stranger to find playmates in a new town. Would've been kinda dull and lonesome without Blacky, I reckon."

"Blacky's as lovable as a hungry rattlesnake, eh, McBean?" Banjo said. "Past month alone he's buried two miners, and last night he plum shot off three fingers from Danny Treleaven's hand."

McBean shrugged and took his seat again. "He's bad news, that Blacky is."

"That's the truth," Banjo said, straightening his wig.

In the ensuing silence, the three men looked away from one another. If Blacky were to return, it would be soon and with fatal results for somebody. Slocum wasn't looking forward to killing a man his first hour in town. Whatever McBean had said to Blacky must have made an impression, though, for he didn't return. At last, Slocum pointed up at the rooms beyond the gallery. "I'm looking for a place to stay overnight. Any of them rooms free?" he asked.

"Don't generally rent them rooms out," Banjo replied.

McBean hoisted his burly body off his stool, towering a good six inches above Slocum. "When he do, stranger," he said with a sneer, "them there rooms get mighty expensive for a night. Banjo here charges by the hour." McBean surveyed Slocum's appearance and added, "By the looks of you, I'd say you might perhaps afford it. But you'll have to go shopping down the street if you're looking for female companionship.

Just go right before Chinatown begins, to Florence's place. Mind you, keep clear of the first room up there," he added grimly, pointing back up at the gallery. "I've got my woman there and I ain't finished with her."

"There're some boardinghouses closer up down the street," Banjo said. "More fitting for sleeping, er, iffin that's what you have a mind fer."

Slocum grinned. "That's good to know. Appreciate you telling me 'bout the sights."

"Take a load off," the bearded giant said, sitting down himself and settling into a comfortable slouch. "You come here to do some prospecting? 'Cause if you did, I can tell you straightaways, you might as well keep on going. There ain't but one good claim here, Gold Hill. Ain't nothing else panned out. There're some sad-faced men moving the worms back and forth for naught. Most men clear out after a few weeks or they start working on Mr. Duncan's Gold Hill."

Slocum pointed at the geese on the table. "Maybe I'll just do some birding, then. Looks like a man ain't liable to starve to death in that line."

"Them critters McBean and I shot this mornin' by the falls," Banjo said, spitting tobacco out of the side of his mouth, into a cuspidor several feet away.

"Banjo here is more of the sportsman than he looks," McBean said, grimacing. "Never fails to bag the bigger bird. What about you? You as handy with the pistol as you are with Banjo's glassware?" McBean nodded toward Slocum's Colt, downing another shot of whiskey.

"Well," Slocum said, leaning into the bar. "The other day I was wondering how I could catch me some fish without getting wet. I was looking down into the water at the fastest salmon you ever saw and I didn't have a pole or gig or anything handy like that. Then I see this osprey eyeing them salmon, too. So I sat still as a rock by the stream and waited, and sure enough that osprey came swoopin' down and clawed up the fastest, juiciest salmon of the school. For one bullet I dined well that night."

"I'll have to try that sometime," McBean said. "Problem is I don't much like fish."

"Then I'd stick to them geese," Slocum said. "They'll make up a nice meal. You say you bagged 'em by the falls?"

"They stop about the falls area every year 'bout this time. You still here next Sunday, you come with Banjo and me."

"Watch out fer them weird squaws by the falls," Banjo put in.

"Them Injuns could strike a man blind if he wasn't prepared for the sight of 'em," McBean said. "What with them dried up udders of theirs. Cover 'em up, I say—six feet under."

"I don't see they do us no harm out of town there in that cave, eh?" Banjo said. "Mebbe not so good fer the bats and vermin is all. But I agree with McBean. I tell ya, they give me the willies." Banjo filled the shot glasses to the brim.

"They said your boy Evan will end up owning the whole damn claim," McBean muttered as he filled up his pipe.

"I can't set no stock in what them crazy Injuns say. You don't neither, do you?"

"Sure I do! First the big one says, 'There's McBean!' She ain't never talked to me, but she uses my name. She says, 'He leads the men who dig for gold.' Then the middle one says, 'The gold will all be his.' Then the last one says, 'The barman Baines's son inherits the gold.'" McBean snorted. "I had a mind to make 'em sorry for bandying about our names like that. You ever talk to em?"

"Never. Ain't that something?" Banjo's blue eyes bulged out at Slocum. "A bit screwy they are, eh? And why, McBean don't have nothin' to do with lookin' after the miners, first off. But look at him now there. He's thinkin' pretty hard about what they said. Wishin' it was true, I'd say." Banjo laughed. "Can't see how McBean can take this serious fer one wishful moment. Mebbe I ain't got no smarts, but I can't picture him leadin' the miners. That was Fletcher's job, it was. Don't look like McBean's cut from the same bolt of cloth as them tenderfeet Eastern boys, to my eye, leastways."

At that moment Evan burst into the saloon. As though driven to contradict his father, he announced, "Old Mr. Duncan wants McBean to replace Mr. Fletcher. Him and Mr. Betcham and Mr. Denahee and the German, too, are all waiting to tell ya, McBean, right over there in the mining office."

McBean paled and raised himself off the stool. "It's like them squaws said. 'McBean, he leads the men in the mines.' " Then the color returned to his face. "Why, I'll be goddamned!" He smirked. "Ain't that somethin'?"

"Another whiskey for McBean, and something for the boy, too," Slocum called to Banjo. "Here's to your good luck!" he toasted.

Banjo poured whiskey for the men and his son, and then he began fidgeting, wiping dust out of the glasses on the shelf. "Congratulations, McBean," he said, rubbing away at an imaginary bit of dirt. "Mebbe you better go see 'em, er, right away, eh? 'Fore they change their minds, iffin they can find 'em."

McBean slapped his fist down so hard on the bar that the entire saloon rattled. He was a big man, almost three hundred pounds of muscle. "Damn right," he said, shoving his wide-brimmed hat over his long, thick hair and showing off a healthy set of teeth. He stomped from the room in boots the size of baby buffaloes.

"I gather this is a real piece of unexpected good fortune," Slocum observed.

"Unexpected? Yes and no. I don't know. Do you, eh?" Banjo murmured. Then, shrugging off his reservations, he added, "I just hope them sisters is right 'bout my busybody son, too." And then he broke into a merry laugh.

"Yep, you sure done raised a good kid there, and he sure seems to know what's about," Slocum said, nibbling on his whiskey.

Evan looked up at the grown men smiling hazily down at him. He didn't really like the taste of his father's whiskey too much, but always drank it when it was offered, even if it did end up giving him the strangest thoughts.

His father's face suddenly lost its merriment. "Boy," he said, "You're covered in mud. What's Mamie gonna say to that, eh? You're liable to get the downside of her boot and nothing to eat, I'd say. It's bad nuff to disrespect the Lord and play in the mud like a heathen on His day, but hellfire and brimstone, you know there's no mercy when it comes to Mamie Jocund. Get upstairs and wash and be quick about it."

Evan had fallen into a mud puddle while eavesdropping on the mining office meeting.

After he'd stabled Slocum's horse, he'd gone back to his father's saloon to see how Slocum was getting on. He'd gone to the back door, which looked past a muddy alley he called Pissmud Lane to the back of the mining office. Just as he was about to creep through the back door, where he could listen in almost as well as by crawling under the floorboards, he'd heard the mining office window across Pissmud Lane open.

Frank Duncan owned the Snake Gulch mine and he scrupulously observed the Sabbath. He even obeyed the missionary ladies who came around in warm weather and said it was a sin to let kids like Evan work in the mine. He was the most religious man Evan had ever met, so it was a real event to have Mr. Duncan at work on the Sabbath.

The office was propped up by stilts to make it somewhat level with the main square it faced. Evan had climbed the stilts to look into the office. And then he'd slipped. And he hated washing up.

Now, covered in mud, he climbed the stairs to the gallery rooms, dejected. Banjo called after him, "Don't you go wakin' and tellin' Angelica." To Slocum, he added, "The women all know everything soon enough, eh?"

Slocum felt confident he had established a rapport with the barkeep. Banjo was the easygoing type that didn't mind talking, and there were some things Slocum needed to know.

Slocum bought Banjo another drink, one he certainly didn't need, before ascertaining where the mining office was and bringing up the other matter on his mind. "I hear there's been some trouble up in these Indian parts."

Banjo nodded sadly. "Injun trouble. There's always that, eh?"

"Even with the Nez Percé? They say they're a right decent tribe," Slocum said, rifling through his saddlebag for tobacco.

"They were right decent at one time. But you can't trust Injuns. Mr. Duncan's taken a tetchy situation indeed and made it right tasty as honey nectar. He gives 'em plenty of business and they leave us alone. Gen'rally speakin', them Nez Percé are damned unlucky to be sittin' on top of all this gold. Ain't that the upside-down way of life with Injuns?"

Slocum offered Banjo a Havana, and they fired them up and listened as rain began pouring down.

Slocum sighed. "I'm strongly attached to those spotted ponies the Nez Percé trade down south a bit," he confessed. "Plan on raising some horses one day and giving up the wild life. Wouldn't suppose there're any Indians doing any horse-trading in these parts."

"A couple Injuns work the stable. They get horses fer Mr. Duncan, no one else. Most all the rest of them Injuns done packed up their tepees and disappeared off someplace else." Then Banjo's eyebrows became rust-colored crescents. "Them weird Injuns is Nez Percé," he cried. "And they seem to know a thing er two. But mebbe they isn't and don't. They don't tan their skins nice like reg'lar Nez Percé. They ain't got no wolf blankets. In fact, they may not be Nez Percé at all, regardless what them stableboys say they is."

"I heard them earlier in the woods right before I got to town," Slocum said. "They said the end was near and, I believe, made reference to the death camases."

"Them mighty weird squaws. Speakin' eerie-like. Not in tongues, I'd say, like them spiritual white folks ya hear about down southways, but, eh, it's not quite normal, three squaws all alone. They've got this perfectly good reservation and the mission at Lapawi—but they refuse to settle down like respectable folks. They got to roam after their buffalo, and Lord knows there ain't many of them left, neither."

"I can understand not wanting to settle down," Slocum admitted.

"It's different fer a young man, of course." Banjo patted Slocum on the arm and measured out a couple shots of whiskey for some more miners drifting in with puffy faces from the previous night's excesses. "I was a young man, too, once, of course. That's the time to do a bit of rovin'. Now I'm settled here fer good. Got me a missus, and though she run off, I'd say she'll be back now the mine's gonna get bigger and the town's gettin' more secure. Them miners of Mr. Duncan's are cuttin' a wide supply road, mebbe finish it by next winter. Now, what was I sayin'? Er, lots of men comin' up here to seek their fortunes, eh? Mr. Duncan pays good wages, but these young men chase gold from place to place like a pack of wolves. Once they get on in years they'll have to be settling down, too. Mebbe not here at the Gulch, but someplace, eh? Every man needs to put down roots in time."

"So you think those Indian ladies are putting down roots here?"

"Ladies?" Banjo laughed, shaking his head at Slocum. "Couldn't say. Mebbe they come here to pass on, like them elephants ya hear about. In Africa, elephants all head off to this one spot when they feel their time comin' on. But, ya know," he said, waving his index finger in the air, "them old squaws are half in the spirit world. What d'ya think about what their predictin' comin' true jes like that? Ain't that somethin'? Mebbe they know a thing or two, after all. And so, mebbe they jes might give you a lead with your ponies."

Banjo waited on a couple more miners, telling them about McBean being named foreman. The miners were clearly happy at the news. When he returned to Slocum, Banjo confessed that he didn't know how to take the news himself.

"I can't say this is a good thing," he said. "Most men ain't fish ner fowl. They in-between like, and you like 'em enough, 'cause, mebbe they're just reg'lar like. But when a man gets hoisted above his nat'ral place and starts to feel like somethin' special, then ye worry. Men like that start actin' foolish, wantin' things, women, they can't rightly afford to keep. You see my point?"

Slocum nodded. He was curious to hear more, but he didn't have to draw Banjo out. The woman in question appeared on the gallery.

She was tall and extremely shapely, a fact emphasized by a tight black corset and bare thighs above cream-colored high-lacing boots. Her sizeable pink breasts undulated as she moved, and the corset's stays were not secured enough to leave much room for imagination.

She had a striking face as well, an imposing nose, black hair that shined like boot polish, ivory skin and teeth, black almond eyes. Her full crimson lips curled in a tight leer as she watched Slocum ogle her.

"Delivery boy!" she called to him in a sharp, raspy voice that filled the room. "Delivery boy! Answer me. Cat got your tongue?"

The room quieted as Slocum swept off his hat. "Miss, you sure are a perty girl, but I'm afraid you've mistaken me for someone else. I'm no delivery boy. Name's John Slocum."

"Too bad," Angelica said, shrugging her fleshy shoulders and turning her back. "I like 'em quick. In and out and no dawdling about. Time is money!" The men in the bar laughed. Angelica made as if to leave, but spun around again. "You sure you're not my delivery boy? You look like a delivery boy and I've been expecting some special mail, some finery to put on my body."

Slocum chuckled under his breath and watched her sashay back out of view. "Nice gal," he said to Banjo.

"That's Angelica. That's about as nice as she gets," he murmured.

Soon Evan crept down the stairs and returned to his father's side.

"That's a good boy," Banjo said, hugging him with one arm. "Take our friend Mr. Slocum to Mamie's with you. She's got a decent place and one of the best kitchens in the territory."

Evan was about to lead Slocum out the back door, because he wanted to eavesdrop on the mining office and hear how McBean was doing, but his father pointed to the swinging doors in front. "Stay outta the mud, you rascal. Take Slocum along the street the direct route."

Outside Evan said, "I thought ya'd like to hear how McBean's doing over by the mining office."

"We can take a look at the office, but just a look-see and then we'd best be getting to the boardinghouse before you get too dirty."

The rain had stopped, leaving the wide, rutted street looking like a riverbed. There were a series of connected porches, but there were also intervals where pedestrians had to step down onto planks laid out over the muddy street.

Evan first led Slocum around the corner to the main square. The few trees about the square were as sorry looking as the antlers decorating Banjo's Saloon. The mining office sat beside a cemetary that bordered a church, which had recently burnt down and was slowly rising from the ashes. Next came a small but sturdy-looking bank. On the other side, Evan pointed out the blacksmith's shop beside the stable. A couple private houses completed the square.

"Who lives in those fancy houses?" Slocum asked.

"Mr. Frank Duncan lives in the big white one."

Slocum whistled through his teeth. "And the other?" He pointed to a smaller, gray frame house on a rise beside Duncan's.

"That was Mr. Fletcher's. He's dead. You think McBean will move in there? His own place is mighty big, but it's halfway up the mountain over yonder. Will I have to call McBean Mr. McBean?" Evan looked at Slocum perplexed.

"If he moves into that gray house, I expect you will." Slocum thought about McBean and the gray house as Evan led him back to the main street. It was hard to imagine the burly mountain man even visiting Fletcher's house, much less living there.

They continued on past a dry goods store, a tailor's shop, and other small businesses, before arriving at the two-story boardinghouse.

Mamie's was jumping compared to the rest of the town. A good twenty-odd miners were sprawled on the porch and milling about the street with plates of hot, steaming food. Evan whispered to Slocum, "Mamie don't let unclean men into her place."

The boy led Slocum into the dining room, where another forty or so men, surprisingly clean for miners, sat on benches around tables laden with plates of hash, cold meats, fried speckled trout, bacon, sweet-smelling pies, and biscuits topped with currant jam. Evan had to push a few of the men out of the way to get through to the kitchen.

There he ran up to a strapping mulatto woman gesticulating to a kitchen staff of seven Chinese men as though she were conducting Beethoven's Ninth. "Mamie," Evan yelled across the din. "This is Mr. Slocum. Paw thought you might have a room for him."

The woman waved her hand left to right to left, saying, "Dinner's three dollars, room's three dollars. That's six dollars total."

"It's a deal," Slocum replied, shaking the hand. "Name's John Slocum."

Mamie smiled, withdrew from his grasp, and held her palm upward. "You're a very fleshly man, aren't you, Mr. Slocum? Now that's six dollars."

Slocum lowered his eyes and coughed. "You've got a nice firm handshake. I like that in a woman." He heard a couple of the cooks snicker as he fumbled in his pockets for the coins.

"Uh-huh, sure. Now, Mr. Slocum, I'm a respectable woman. If you want to hold hands or satisfy your other carnal desires, there is an establishment in Snake Gulch that caters to just that sort of thing. That's your business, not mine. Here we eat and sleep and we keep the dirt outside. Fat Sang will take your saddlebags and show you your room."

Evan already had a plate of food in his hands when Slocum looked down at him. "Son," he said, "gonna drop my stuff off in the room and then go out for a bit. So if I miss you, I'll see you later at your pa's. Okay?"

The boy was disappointed. He wouldn't be able to show Slocum off to his friends, and Clint and the other kids were just coming in. "You will come around later, Slocum, won't you?"

Slocum promised and went to see his room. It looked out on the street, and from his window he could see Blacky lurking beside the funeral parlor. Probably picking out his casket, Slocum thought. That man was as hell-bent to die as any loser to cross his path.

Slocum retraced his way back to the mining office just in time to see McBean rounding his way back to the saloon. Slocum rapped on the office door and went in.

"I've come from Gary Clarkson in Lewiston," he said to a well-preserved, white-haired man. "Mr. Duncan, I presume?"

"You've made it in good time," the man replied, and turned to his men sitting around the boardroom table. "Gentlemen, our deed has returned."

Slocum reached into the breast pocket under his jacket and produced the rolled parchment.

"He carries the deed like I do," Duncan said, taking the paper and slipping it inside his vest. "Close to the good heart."

Slocum could think of safer places for a rich man to keep his valuables, but it wasn't for him to complain. There seemed to be something peculiar going on in Snake Gulch. This roomful of thin, light-haired men holding themselves so properly seemed at odds with the rough town. Their expensive suits and polished shoes looked dangerously vulnerable. Slocum would be happy to move along as soon as he got a bit of sleep.

Duncan introduced him to his men around the table: the bank president and mine treasurer, William Betcham; the architect, Donal Denahee; and the geologist, Wolfgang Schmidt.

"Fletcher stole this deed from me," Duncan explained to Slocum. "It is my special dispensation from the territorial governor to work on Indian land. Fletcher left us purportedly to deliver a gold shipment to our bank. Now he's a-hanging in Lewiston."

"A fitting and foul end for the thief," Denahee interjected.

"Aye, he swings sweetly in the bitter April breezes," Duncan agreed. "Far better he'd a been had he rubbed his eyes and wakened from his wicked dreams. Better we'd all be . . . And blind as heathens we were to trust that man, for he must always ha' been pretendin' to love us. As wee laddies, Mr. Denahee, you sat with him close as nestling birdies in that great university in New Haven. And I like a father to you both. My food was yours, my gold I shared freely with all of you.

"Now we are richer all of us in gold and for bein' rid of his deceitful, treacherous ways. Rich we are in the knowledge of his true character, yet now that he is nae more, we, too, are poorer. We ha' lost a dear part of our past; our memories of daylight cheer are colors, fool's gold. Lord ha' mercy on his soul—and ours."

Slocum looked at the solemn expressions on Betcham, Denahee, and Schmidt's faces. They seemed in perfect sympathy with the old man's words.

After a horrible minute of silence, Duncan continued. "The deed to Gold Hill is inscribed with my name on it and I ha' grown rich off it. Rich as Croesus, as will all you fine gentlemen—and before you reach my age. A fair, more than fair, portion of our treasure already goes to you, as well. You own your piece of the hill. After my death you will share the deed between yourselves. Is that not fair?"

Duncan's voice had grown hoarse. Denahee tried to interject something, but Duncan raised a hand to stop him. "Mr. Fletcher shall not succeed in undoing my faith in man," he said. "To keep smellin' the roses in God's air, this ol' man must believe the rest of you ha' love for me. You are my wee birdies—my memory. The other one crept in by pretense. For Mr. Fletcher seized our gold not out of greed, but out of hatred. Hatred I say! He was the serpent hiding in our nest . . . an evil acolyte of the devil himself."

The men gasped, and Duncan assumed a more businesslike mien, gesturing to Slocum. "This trustworthy man was sent to bring us the deed from the authorities in Lewiston," he said. "Now order is restored and the deed returned unto my person. And our winter's gold, Mr. Betcham, is safe in the strong banks at Walla Walla. I heard this report last night. The glad tidings were borne on the swift feathers of our good Indian brothers, as was the news of the justice served to the scoundrel."

Slocum shifted uneasily on his feet, and Duncan continued. "The brave Mr. McBean shall replace Mr. Fletcher. He has accepted to meet the challenges of the job with equanimity. His loyalty and shrewdness are more than proven. It was he who told us what Mr. Fletcher had done, at a time when we were loath to think ill of Mr. Fletcher—yet timely still for us to revise our thinking and catch him.

"We always wanted a strong man to manage the workers; now we ha' someone from the workers. A good, stout man, Mr. McBean. With the stamp mill comin' on soon and a new beginning at hand, he will be most valuable in judgin' the fittest men to send into the depths of our tunnels. Most important, yea, he knows his place and we can trust his loyalty to us."

Duncan turned to Slocum. "Mr. Slocum," he said, handing him a purse of gold coins. "We could use a swift and honorable man like you in Snake Gulch. We need protection transporting our gold to the big banks. We have another shipment ready now. Would you consider staying with us for a while?"

Slocum held the purse in his palm. It weighed more than Clarkson had promised. He pocketed it with a grin. Good old Clarkson had come through. Now he had enough money to take care of himself for a while, maybe start his horse farm. "I'm afraid I have other commitments," he said to Duncan, building his corral in his mind.

Duncan bowed slightly to him, and feeling dismissed, Slocum said his good-byes and left the office.

Heading back to Mamie's, he felt less happy than he had expected. And he was weighed down by more than the gold. It was as though the whole town were watching him. He had spotted Blacky in back of the mining office, where apparently he'd been eavesdropping. And, framed in the second-floor window of Banjo's Saloon, he saw McBean and Angelica looking down at him. He didn't like the expression on their faces one bit.

2

The air had a faint odor of rotten eggs. Slocum looked about his little room. He would stretch out on the bed for five minutes, finish eating, and push off. If he got too tired to make it through to Lewiston, he'd sleep under the stars. That would be far better than getting used to the grim sights, smells, and people of Snake Gulch.

He pulled his hat down, closed his eyes, and opened them again to the inside of the Stetson. The velvety darkness always brought back memories of Mary Jane and the wild times they'd had in Kansas City. When she presented him with the black Stetson their last night together, she suggested he cover his eyes with it on the lonely road, and dream of her until they met again. It was an open invitation.

After dreaming a bit about Mary Jane, Slocum lifted himself off the rickety bed and looked out the window to the street below. It was getting dark. He'd shut his eyes a lot longer than he'd supposed.

Blacky was gone and no one else was spying up at his window. Slocum picked absentmindedly at the plate of food he'd carried up to the room but been too tired to eat. Now the food was cold, and there was a funny smell. Maybe not the food, and not the sulfur odor from the mine, either. He'd been riding a long time and would have to shuck off his jeans real

22

soon, he realized, before the worn denim fused to his sweaty skin. He'd made that mistake already a couple of times and was not especially keen on repeating the experience.

It was too late to start back to Lewiston. Slocum dreaded having to coax the mulish roan down the steep mountain path in the dark. A quick trot out to the falls, however, would be possible before dark. He could ask those prophetic old Indian sisters about his chances of rustling up some ponies, though he didn't expect the kind of supernatural help Banjo had thought he might get there. The sisters might know where the Nez Percé were doing their horse-trading, though, so Slocum could head out that way in the morning.

The rejuvenating nap hadn't helped dispel his uneasiness about the mining town. He would follow his gut and quit it at the first opportunity.

Slocum made his way back to the main square to retrieve his roan from the stable and to hear what the stable hands had to say. The two young men working there, Matthew and Elk Dog, chatted about the rough winter they'd just weathered and other sundry small talk. They didn't betray the faintest interest in Slocum. Slocum was grateful. He didn't cotton to folks who asked too many questions. His own question was a simple one, but he didn't want to seem in too great a hurry. If they had any horseflesh to sell, he wanted to strike a good bargain, after all. But there was a limit to discretion. The stable hands seemed actively to avoid discussing any subject of substance.

The Nez Percé had always enjoyed an especially close and friendly relationship with the white man. Friendly, that is, until recently, when Young Chief Joseph refused to cede to the United States land which his dying father had made him swear never to relinquish.

Slocum tried to broach this subject, reminiscing about the time he'd met Old Chief Joseph, but the Indians immediately shifted topics. Finally, Slocum recalled the name the Nez Percé went by among their own people. "Nimipu?" he asked Elk Dog, motioning toward the young man's hair, which was styled in the tribe's traditional fashion.

For an awkward moment, Elk Dog glared suspiciously at Slocum. Then he walked out the back doors to the corral. Slocum was annoyed at himself for his gaffe. If these men had anything he was interested in, he'd just set himself back days in negotiations. This was a bad beginning, and he wasn't desperate enough to make good on such a start. Yet he was curious what his mistake had been. If he were going to the three-river juncture down south, he'd better know what not to do. "I say something to upset him?" he asked Matthew.

"Few white men call us by our name," Matthew said earnestly. "It means 'the people,' and it is an idea we hold sacred. But now the white man has invoked our name to divide our people. The white man says the chiefs who signed their treaties signed for Nimipu."

Slocum shrugged. He'd have to remember not to use that word when approaching the horse traders down south. He could tell bargaining with Matthew would not be easy. As for the different divisions of the Nez Percé, Slocum would never be able to distinguish between the dozens of different groups.

The Indian continued. "Don't be angry at Elk Dog. He doesn't trust the white man. Unless he knows him well, like Mr. Duncan. I know you mean no harm. I can see that in your face. You are not false like many of your people. They have divided our people. They have taken away our ancestral lands. We are divided and we have lost much of our land. This is a bad time for us."

Slocum couldn't disagree. He thought of the hoarse voice saying the end was near. He assured Matthew that he was not interested in his land.

"Maybe not," Matthew replied. "But the sins of your leaders come back to haunt you."

"I hope not all your people feel that way! I was thinkin' of buying some spotted ponies down south by the convergence of the Weiser, Payette, and Boise rivers. Your people still trade horses there, don't they?"

"No, we do not trade horses as freely as before. Mr. Duncan buys many of our people's horses when we need to sell for money. Our men need horses badly now, and we only sell horses as a last resort . . . when we need money, or other things we cannot get with money." Matthew looked serenely at Slocum, adding, "Elk Dog and I must bring Mr. Duncan's horses in. Come and you can see them."

Slocum was not encouraged, but he hadn't given up hope. He had the sense that Matthew had something for him to see. He followed the small, lean Indian out back. From behind Matthew could have been taken for a white man. His hair was cut short and his duds were the same of any horse handler. One of the traditional benefits of buying from the Nez Percé was the directness of negotiations. Slocum gathered that this was another of the old ways that Matthew had set aside.

There were half a dozen Appaloosas fenced in on a wide run. In a smaller corral beside it, Elk Dog was talking into the ear of a proud silvery stallion, who seemed so erect and intelligent he appeared to comprehend whatever Elk Dog was telling him.

It was obvious at first glance that the big stallion with the flint-colored eyes was what Slocum was being led out to see. He was a remarkable horse; at once massive and defiant, and then, with a flick of his long silver tail, he seemed ethereal and weightless.

"These are Mr. Duncan's mountain horses," Matthew said, gesturing away from the silver stallion, at the Appaloosas.

Slocum was willing to play the game for a while. "That wild mustang belong to Duncan, too?" His tone was decidedly derisive.

Matthew seemed not to notice, however, and gazed at the stallion with reverence. "Our people call him the Ghost Horse. He is a legend in these parts, and no, he does not belong to Mr. Duncan. He cannot be owned. His spirit is indomitable."

Slocum raised his eyebrows. "Hasn't been broken yet?"

Matthew smiled. "Elk Dog has trained him well, but he has a violent nature. He once commanded a large herd of wild horses that ran under the moon. The other horses were all captured first, and when the Ghost Horse was finally brought in, he couldn't be left in the company of other horses. He's killed a couple of them since. That's why he has his own corral."

"That is unusual. Ain't heard of a horse that kills its own before. Does he kill the fillies, too?"

As though overhearing them, the Ghost Horse whinnied in a low register at the word "fillies."

"He likes the fillies," Matthew said.

"Reckon even a horse that can't be owned can still be sold." Slocum didn't want to appear too taken with the stallion, however, so he shifted the conversation to the other Indians in the Gulch. "What about those old sisters at the falls? I hear they're from your people. Do they deal horses?"

"They have no horses. And if they did, they would not sell to you. I don't know the sisters, but I have heard of them from others. They mourn the passing of the old ways. I am a Christian, and I believe the old ways will not last. Reverend Spalding at Lapawi taught me well. I trade horses to the white man to help my people live for tomorrow. Our people are frightened, defenseless. They have little protection. Few guns."

At last Slocum felt he was making progress. "Few guns? Why, I have a Henry Repeating rifle I'd be willing to trade for a passal of fine-looking ponies. I'd hate to part with it. Gotten me out of several terrible fixes and I'm mighty sentimental."

"A good rifle, but one Henry is not enough to protect our people." Matthew was stoney-faced, uncompromising. He pointed toward the Ghost Horse. "The stallion is worth four Henrys."

Slocum laughed. "No horse is worth four rifles, Matthew. And besides, that wild mustang ain't worth a slingshot. Who'd want a murderous horse?"

"We must bring the horses in," Matthew said. "It is growing dark and Mr. Duncan likes his own to be brought in early. The night is full of bad spirits." Matthew went to the large corral, signaling Elk Dog to join him.

Slocum kicked up some dirt and nonchalantly moved over to admire the silver stallion. Someday that horse would make a corral full of fillies pretty darn happy, he thought. He'd get Matthew to trade the stallion for his Henry, even if he was worth four. Slocum only had one rifle, but the Indian seemed desperate for any arms he could get. It would just require a bit of patience. And judging from the horse's high, prancing step and graceful carriage, the negotiating time would pay off. Slocum would give himself a week, but if he played his hand right, he might be able to cut loose of the Gulch a bit earlier than that. The key to the strategy would be to seem to have all the time in the world. They shouldn't suspect that he was itching to move on.

The pall that hung over the town had not lifted at night's onset. But despite the gloom Slocum felt rested and a bit encouraged. The Ghost Horse was a splendid beast, and the beast was within his reach. As he walked around the square to the main street, his mind wandered from his plans to musings about the fleshpots of Snake Gulch.

Whistling, he ambled toward Florence's cathouse, only to be waylaid by Evan.

"Slocum! Slocum!" the boy cried, running down the street.

"Evan," Slocum replied, coming to a halt and turning to the boy with surprise. "What's the trouble?"

"It's . . ." The boy shivered. "It's Paw's man, Paulie, the barman. He's in a heap of trouble with Blacky. They're at it right now. Ya gotta come save him. Ya gotta. He ain't got no gun and Blacky's aimin' to shoot him down."

The boy beckoned Slocum back toward Banjo's. Slocum sighed. Evan's big blue eyes were swelled with tears, but he held them back. Slocum didn't know what to tell the boy, but he certainly didn't think it his place to interfere in some dispute between Banjo's barman and Blacky.

"Reckon there ain't much I can do," he admitted as gently as he could. "I'm a stranger here, Evan. Can't go sticking my nose in other people's fights. Ain't there someone else you can get to step in?"

"No. There's no one. Ya gotta stop him. Paulie don't even got a gun."

Looked like Slocum would have to postpone meeting the ladies for now. "Okay, I'll come with you. But I ain't gonna interfere in their fight. I don't know what I can do," Slocum said in a kindly voice, "but I'll come along with you and I'll make sure they don't do you no harm."

As he walked through the batwings, he saw the saloon owner look at him with relief. Blacky was making unkind remarks about Paulie's parentage, and Paulie was bawling like a babe. Then, suddenly, Banjo raised a bottle and broke it over his barman's head.

Blacky shot off a couple rounds in the air. "You lily-livered skunk, Banjo," he cried. "You ruin my fun. But I can still kill that man, cain't I? Even if he ain't able to notice it, cain't I still kill him?"

The men at Blacky's table guffawed. They thought he was a real stitch. A great guy, until he turned on one of them, Slocum thought.

"My gun's hungry for blood," Blacky snarled, aiming his Smith & Wesson at various miners here and there in the barroom. But soon his face lost its anger and the men around him resumed their poker game. Blacky didn't look at Slocum as he passed his table, but Slocum knew the mustachioed miner had caught a glimpse of him. Cowardly, or had someone told him to back off? Slocum couldn't be sure.

Evan bent over the unconscious barman next to his father. Slocum figured while he was there he'd order himself a whiskey. He told Banjo he could wait till Banjo had checked his barman's vital signs.

"I, ugh, could use a hand with ol' Paulie here," Banjo replied.

Slocum swung the barman over his shoulder and followed Banjo to a small upstairs room. After flopping Paulie down on the mattress, Slocum felt a stinging pain in his shoulder and imagined a pair of pretty hands kneading out the soreness. "Guess I'll be pushing off, Banjo. Glad to be of help."

"My man Paulie here'll be all right come a day er two. Guess I hit him a mite harder than necessary, eh? But that dang fool was getting all nervous by Blacky's, er, sense of humor."

"I don't cotton much to it, either." Slocum eyed Banjo sternly.

"It's part of the job here, it is. In the Gulch there's always a Blacky comin' in regular-like. And a barman who ain't man enough to deal with 'em Blackys of the world better go running on back to his mama's house, eh?"

"Be a good deal fairer to send the Blackys packing instead," Slocum observed.

Banjo wiped his brow, his eye twinkling. "Fair? What's fair out here? Ain't nobody here to enforce fairness. Tell me, John, you've got a steady hand and a sharp eye. Why don't you work fer me, eh? Fer a while at least. I sure could use a strong, sensible young feller like yourself."

"Better get a man who's fixin' to hunker down longer than a week—'cause that's all the time I plan to stay at the Gulch."

Banjo had untied the barman's apron and now halfheartedly presented it to Slocum as though it were a modest bouquet proffered to a lady. "When I saw you coming in I thought you'd surely fill in fer tonight, eh?" he whined. "Tonight's sure to be tough without another set of hands, and I hate to ask my boy Evan to fill in. The boy needs his sleep, but I cain't be handling the bar alone. Nope, that's impossible. My hands aren't as quick as they used to be and the men get mighty nasty when I'm slow."

Slocum could only think to suggest that Banjo close the joint down for the night. Just as he was about to suggest as much, Angelica slipped into the room, wrapped in a scarlet silk dress with two thick hubs jutting out, her nipples pressed against the fabric. She sniffed and sat on the edge of the bed beside the unconscious barman, stroking his bloodied forehead. "Paulie was such a dear."

"He'll be fine in a couple days," Slocum said to console her, his eyes rivited to her bosom.

Angelica stood up abruptly. "What?" she cried, her hand lifting off the man's skin. "He's alive?"

Banjo nodded proudly. "Blacky was gonna blast him away—and Paulie didn't even have a gun on him—but I smacked him over the head with a bottle before Blacky could do more damage than that."

"Good. You made a fool of Blacky," Angelica said, pursing her lips. "I can just imagine him holding out his gun and having nothing to shoot at. But I'm surprised he didn't shoot you in Paulie's stead, Banjo Baines."

"Blacky's crazy. Dangerous crazy. There's no stopping him when he gets itchin' fer bloodshed. Er, I wouldn't be surprised to learn he'd taken your pretty face off your head, neither."

"Banjo!" Slocum objected. "Is that a way to talk to a lady?"

"I can't have that madman popping my men off," Banjo yelled back at Slocum. "If it warn't fer Blacky's day bein' surely numbered, I'd've taken it into my head to do something about him, I tell you."

"Well," Slocum snarled, "you could keep him out of your darn saloon for starters."

"McBean wouldn't like that," Angelica snapped. She lowered her lashes flirtatiously at Slocum. "McBean's fond of Blacky, likes to have him around. He makes McBean laugh."

"Oh, he's the life of the party, I'm sure," Slocum said, heading to the door.

"You know what's good for you, Mr. Big Bad Gunfighter, you keep out of Blacky's way."

Slocum couldn't tell whether Angelica was egging him on or really trying to scare him off. A moment earlier nothing short of a natural catastrophe could have kept Slocum from Florence's courtesans. And yet in that moment, his desire for female companionship had shriveled to nothing. He took the apron still clutched in Banjo's grasp. "I'll fill in for Paulie, if you still want me to." Anyway, having a job would help convince the Indians he wasn't going to rush the negotiations.

Banjo was happy, but not quite surprised by this stroke of good fortune. "Don't go pickin' no fights with Blacky, now," he warned in a light tone, patting Slocum on the back.

"Banjo, if I do, don't you dare whack me like you did Paulie. I can hold my own."

Angelica smiled. "You men are all such little boys," she teased. "You never listen to advice from the female sex. In fact, you all do just the opposite. Luckily, we're good for more than advice, Slocum. So don't be a stranger, Mr. Barman, Mr. Gunfighter, my slow-coming delivery boy. Drop by Florence's if you find a moment or two. I'll introduce you around to the girls. Of course, I won't have the pleasure of entertaining you personally." Angelica flung her hand out for Baines and Slocum to see. "I'm engaged. McBean just now proposed to me."

There was no further trouble from Blacky and his quarter that evening. In the small hours of the night, after the last miner had collapsed under his table and Slocum was finally able to untie his apron, he realized he was too tired to head off to Flo's for a nightcap. Instead, Slocum returned to his wobbly, chaste bed at Mamie's and didn't even give Mary Jane a thought before being reduced to snores.

The slow and predictable patterns of life in Snake Gulch soon engulfed Slocum. Daily life revolved around the shifts at the mine, and talk of the mine was all he heard at the saloon.

The miners working Duncan's claim were busy at a multitude of tasks up at Gold Hill. Small accidents accounted for most of the miners' shoptalk, but there was also much speculation about new shafts being sunk and rumors that new machinery was going to arrive soon, coming from Nevada and California by pack mule.

The town's attention revolved around the survival of the mine, for it was the lifeblood of Snake Gulch. So many other towns in the territory had folded up like a bad hand the moment their mines stopped paying top dollar—and this was something many of the miners in Snake Gulch knew from firsthand experience. The shopkeepers and miners alike looked to Duncan for reassurance, and Duncan promised them a glorious future.

Slocum saw a bit of that optimistic old man when they crossed paths as Slocum paid his daily half-hour visits to the stable hands. Slocum didn't give Duncan much attention. The old man was fired with a vision of Snake Gulch as the booming metropolis it would be in the future. He was an eccentric, but Slocum could see why he was so popular in the town. Despite his white hair, his face seemed unnaturally unlined for his age, as though time refused to leave its mark on him in its customary way. And the man's cheeks were perpetually colored with flaming red circles like a clown's. He was jolly and friendly and never failed to reiterate his offer of employment to Slocum.

Slocum, however, was determined to quit Snake Gulch as soon as he acquired the Ghost Horse. As of Thursday he'd gotten the Indians to agree, in principle at least, that one Henry was worth more to their people than a wild horse with a reputation that daunted most of their braves. It was only a matter of a day or two, Slocum figured, before he would be able to translate the principle into a firm deal. All that remained to settle was how much ammunition Slocum would have to throw in, but Matthew was in no great rush to finalize negotiations. "When we are out of cartridges, what good will the rifle do our people?" he'd asked more than once. Apparently the townspeople were reluctant to sell gunpowder to the Indians.

Slocum had worked all week at Banjo's, because Paulie rode out of town the very day he regained consciousness and there were no other takers for the job. Slocum found the situation perplexing. He suspected that Blacky was throwing his weight about trying to intimidate prospective replacements. There was some reason Blacky had for wanting him behind the bar. Maybe it was just for the challenge.

It was amusing to have someone as transparent as Blacky studying him, waiting for a chance that would never come. It also kept Slocum on his toes, though. He always had to know where the mustachioed miner was and what trouble he was up to when he came round the saloon. Three times Slocum had to drive shot glasses into Blacky's forehead. After that, Blacky gave up direct confrontations, and dealing with him became fun. Occasionally Slocum would make an offhand remark about which ace was up Blacky's sleeve, exciting not much in the way of a response from Blacky. While the hell-raiser did his best to bare his teeth and curse like a demon, in the end he always deferred to Slocum's authority.

McBean, meanwhile, was out of the picture. His new responsibilities kept him busy overseeing the miners by day. At night, he and Angelica were off at his house in the hills, sprucing up the place for their wedding celebration.

The nuptuals were set for Friday night, and the lovebirds had invited the entire town. While the miners drinking at the saloon didn't talk about the wedding at all, except to assert that it was going to be a real occasion, Slocum heard of nothing but from Mamie back at the boardinghouse. She was in charge of the food, and the prospect of feeding three hundred hungry miners was almost as daunting as the money she expected to get thrilled her.

Banjo had been offered exclusive rights to dispense his wares at the fete. Apparently, McBean was paying him a king's ransom, for Banjo in turn had asked Slocum to help pour whiskey at the party and offered as much gold as Duncan had paid for the return of his deed. Now that McBean was an officer at the gold mine, gold meant nothing to him. It seemed the closer to the source you got, the less it was worth.

Slocum didn't mind. He'd be riding out of the Gulch with a good stud horse and two bags heavy with enough gold to start working his own horse ranch in style. Not bad for a week's work, he would think on occasion. Then he would push the thought out of his mind. It was too easy. And the one thing Slocum could never get used to trusting was easy money.

On the day of the wedding, Slocum awoke as usual sometime a little after noon. Mamie's place was a flurry of activity as mule after mule was loaded with pots and pans and sent off into the mountains, to McBean's. Slocum went to the stable to catch a glimpse of the flint-eyed stallion, but the Indians were too preoccupied to talk. At Banjo's the bar owner was busy mixing up whiskey in large quantities.

"This is the craziest notion I ever heard," he said to Slocum. "Why, McBean's place ain't hardly in Snake Gulch. And he wants me to tote up enough liquor for three hundred miners! It's a good five miles across a dang winding Injun trail. Reckon Angelica jes wants to make it difficult for her sister, the widder, to come. But Lordy if it ain't gonna be hard work fer me."

"You fixin' to lock up the saloon for the wedding?" Slocum asked.

"Reckon everybody'll be hiking on up to McBean's. People like him and the drinks are all on him. But I ain't never closed my saloon fer one day. Evan will mind it fer his paw," Banjo said. "I'll be takin' my tent on up to McBean's, the original one I used when I first opened up in Orofino. I'll just set up that tent like I did when Snake Gulch warn't nothing but a bunch of trees, eh, Evan? McBean says he's gonna make me a rich man iffin I keep the liquor flowin' at that weddin' of his, and I've a hankering to get rich today!"

"Nice having friends in high places," Slocum observed.

"They're all big shots till they're fired. Speakin' on which, I surely could use a hand with them there kegs."

Evan wanted to go to the wedding, and kept looking up with hope brimming in his trusting blue eyes. He didn't use them to plea, though, and Slocum appreciated his restraint as he dutifully loaded up Banjo's mules. He wasn't going to tell the man how to be a good father.

Slocum and Banjo were among the first to arrive at McBean's, though by the time they had strung up the tent, more than a hundred thirsty men had appeared. In no time the free alcohol was flowing like the great Missouri.

"Let's just fill up the trough with whiskey," Slocum suggested.

Banjo considered the idea seriously for a minute. "Don't suppose that would be right fittin' fer a weddin'," he replied at last.

The bride did not wear white, but she didn't wear harlot red, either. Seeing her alight from her horse, decked out in a pearl-gray suit as fine as any worn in New York or Paris, Slocum couldn't help but whistle under his breath.

Banjo pointed at the damsels from Flo's bordello, who followed Angelica into the glen. "Jes look at 'em outfits them bridesmaids is wearin'," he said. "Them there womenfolk are lookin' fer business more than they're givin' away their girlfriend, eh?"

For six nights Slocum had hoped to visit Flo's, only to find himself too weary to care by evening's end. Maybe he just hadn't got used to the poor quality of air at the Gulch. He now saw what he'd been missing and was hard put to concentrate on pouring Banjo's wash.

McBean's place was a sizeable lodge, with several bedrooms. Slocum discovered that McBean had gotten lucky for a time with his own placer and had built the house with the idea that he could keep a team of his own men working it. Just as he finished the house, though, the vein turned bad on him. Still, he was proud of his acre and wouldn't move to town.

The hurdy-gurdy man who'd come with the bridesmaids moved the party to a new level of noise and excitement, but stopped in the middle of "The Gypsy Davy" because, Slocum saw, Frank Duncan had arrived at last.

He came up the path in between the two Indians Matthew and Elk Dog, treating them like personal servants. It appeared that without them he'd have been unable to get off his horse.

A hush fell over the crowd as all present craned their necks to see Duncan shake McBean's hand. McBean summoned the preacher, Laboite, whom Banjo had just revived, and the marriage ceremony was hurriedly performed before the preacher passed out for good.

Then the music began again, and the crowd chimed in:

> There was a lord, a highborn lord
> He married a highborn lady
> She up and left her bed and board
> And eloped with the Gypsy Davy
> Ri too ral loo ral loo ral lay
> Beware of the Gypsy Lady . . .

The drinks were flowing faster than ever.

"Them women dance dern nice, eh?" Banjo observed. "They come reg'lar to the saloon on Fridays and Saturdays and get themselves a dollar a dance from their men. But look at 'em dancin' fer free. I ain't never seen that before in this town."

Each of Angelica's bridesmaids was keeping ten to twenty men dancing at the same time. They spun about into one man's arms and off into the next one's before any of the miners were able to catch hold of them. Florence, the platinum-blonde maid of honor, held Slocum's gaze for a moment and moved her tongue over her lips provocatively.

"Weddings always seemed to me to be a good place to meet eligible young ladies," Slocum commented.

"Them women aren't fer me, mind you," Banjo murmured. "I've got my missus. Time being, she's up in Lewiston with her people." With a sigh, he added, "Said she couldn't handle bein' snowed in another winter. Said she couldn't handle keepin' the boy outter trouble. Said she had no use fer the minin' life, no more. She went to stay with her cousins in October."

Slocum had heard Banjo relate the tale of his desertion several times before. Each retelling was unique in both fact and emphasis. Only the pathos remained the same.

Banjo brightened. "She just hates the dark winter months. Needs street lamps and high society and all. She's a fine-lookin' woman, and well bred, too. I'm nowheres near good 'nuff fer her, but now that the snows are gone, I expect her back any day. She loves springtime in the mountains, and she knows her boy is missin' her. I know it in my bones, that she'll be back."

The crowd had grown quiet again, and all the men under Banjo's tent went out to hear Duncan toast the couple.

"Men," he cried out, "and lovely lassies. God has opened his rosy gardens up to Mr. McBean today. A man McBean is of long vision and keen understanding. A brawny man he is and a God-fearing, honest man he is, too. What, ye ask, is God's reward for such a man? No greater one could thar be but the love of a bonny lassie. But nae ordinary lass has he caught up in his net. Nae, I say, for I have eyes in my head, and ye know, too, I exaggerate na to say she is as lovely as a goddess."

The crowd hooted rudely. Duncan blushed at some of the language the men used. "Laddies," he cried, good-naturedly beaming at the crowd. "Thar be ladies present."

Some of the drunken miners howled uncontrollably. One of the more romantic bridesmaids in the back shouted out, "Yeah, if McBean can make a lady out of one of us, you other mole men can."

"Who's gonna go courting whores?" one tough remarked, and a small fracas broke out.

Duncan raised his hands, and peace was eventually restored. "Mr. McBean labored beside ye, and now he has my ear," Duncan called out. "Use it to speak to me. Mr. Fletcher is nae more and Mr. McBean's star has risen."

The men all drew their pistols and shot off their rounds into the air. Duncan and the wedding party hastened into the house.

Banjo and Slocum returned to the whiskey tent. "Reckon they're gonna want their wine," Banjo said, pouring a yellowish liquid from a keg into several jugs. "Look to you like wine, eh?" he asked.

"Sure," Slocum said. "But it don't much look like grape wine."

"Er, it ain't exactly," Banjo admitted. "Look here, do you mind toting this here grapeless wine and this vintage Taos

Lightnin' to the house? I reckon the fine newlyweds are gonna need a barman keeping their guests in the house happy. It'll be crazy back here, and I can't be paintin' tonsils in but one place at a time."

Slocum had to step on some toes to get through the doorway of McBean's house. Seemed like everyone was at the doorstep wanting to look inside.

Yet once he was past the doorway and inside, it was relatively uncongested. Just a handful of miners, an equal number of merchants, and the men Slocum recognized from Duncan's office. Angelica was pouring tea for Duncan when she spotted Slocum. "At last, my delivery boy has arrived," she sang out merrily to the crowd, who got a laugh at his expense.

"Congratulations, ma'am," Slocum said, settling his jugs and bottles down and dipping his hat her way.

Angelica came over to Slocum, still holding the teapot, and spoke quietly, almost conspiratorially. At first Slocum thought she was arranging a future assignation, but her voice was devoid of flirtation.

"Mr. Duncan does not drink alcohol, but the rest of these fine men shouldn't have to be asked if their glass needs topping."

Slocum cleared his throat.

Angelica continued. "Don't get all huffy. You'll do what I tell you to. It's my wedding day, for the Lord's sake. Oh, I know you're much too important to be doing this sort of lowly service work."

"Guess I should be grateful that it's not your wedding day too often," Slocum said, keeping the banter light. He set about filling glasses, cups, and jars with whiskey, still reeling from Angelica's caustic tone.

McBean was a huge presence in the midst of the contingent of large mining men. The others were more spread about the room. Betcham and Schmidt didn't take any notice of Slocum, but Denahee nodded his head in recognition.

"You are a versatile man, Mr. Slocum," he said. He never came into Banjo's Saloon, so this was his first sight of Slocum since Slocum returned Duncan's deed. "Is this the commitment you spoke of earlier?" Slocum shook his head, smiling. "Are you planning to stay the summer in Snake Gulch?"

"Ain't met one of you Snake Gulchers that's been here more than three years, but you all keep wondering if I plan to stay. Is there something I'm missing?"

"People are afraid of men like you," Denahee said, surprising Slocum with his directness. "People would rather have gunslingers like you stay in town where they can keep an eye on you. Bad men go roving about these hills, lying in wait for lone prospectors and for our gold shipments to Lewiston. Bad men like you, or those two over there." Denahee nodded his head toward two men wearing black Stetsons like Slocum's, pausing before the open doorway before moving on.

"That thief Fletcher you heard about—he used to be a good man. But when we get snowbound, we can't work, and there's not much recreation. A winter up here can change a man. Now, I expect Mr. McBean will have a trying time coming up with a trustworthy man to take our next gold shipment to Walla Walla. Can't do it himself. He'll be too busy handling the men."

"That's very interesting, but as I said before . . . other commitments." Slocum continued about the room pouring whiskey. He didn't want to think about the trouble in store for Snake Gulch. He'd be gone tomorrow.

Just as he got to thinking about Matthew and Elk Dog, he saw the Indians come into the room and move toward Duncan. Angelica headed them off.

She called for Slocum. "Please find some glasses for our Indian brothers, Mr. Slocum."

"We can't stay, Miss—Mrs. McBean, ma'am," Matthew said. "It's going to be dark soon and we must get Mr. Duncan home."

"Nonsense!" Angelica laughed. "Mr. Duncan must stay for dinner." Turning toward the old man, she added, "And Mr. Duncan just got here. He must rest before heading back. You do look a wee bit tired, Mr. Duncan. More tea? Are you feeling ill?"

Duncan shook his head and shifted in his chair as though trying unsuccessfully to stand.

Matthew managed to move past Angelica to Duncan's side. "We will take you back now, before it gets dark."

Duncan looked up at the young man, his pale eyes unfocused and his lips trembling. "Uncommonly, unnaturally tired am I," he said, sinking down in his chair. "I must rest."

"Oh, Slocum, what are we to do?" Angelica whispered. "Go to the kitchen and ask Mamie to make sure a room is ready for Mr. Duncan. It looks like he will need to lie down before dinner."

Slocum ambled off to the kitchen, happy to escape the wedding party and even happier to find Mamie ordering her helpers about as efficiently as she managed her own kitchen.

"Mrs. McBean has made me a right rich woman today," Mamie said. "Though I do kind of hate taking all her savings. I know she just wore her back out working all winter long for that gold. But I reckon now she's married, she's done retired. Probably don't like the sight of that gold, remembering where it came from."

Slocum looked out the window at three deer turning on spits. "I see you're fixin' up some venison," he remarked.

"Mrs. McBean ordered me to feed the town with no time to order proper provisions. But then again, she ain't a proper lady herself. So I've had my people shoot anything that moves. Don't matter what it is, I'll be serving it. Them deer is just the beginning. Out back I have five more Chinamen fixin' up some mighty exotic dishes."

Slocum delivered his message. Mamie rolled her eyes. "It's that flowery tea she made for him that's tiring him out," she said. "Lord knows she can't boil water, but she insists on making his tea herself. And I tell you, I had a taste of it, and I can't hardly think proper, I'm so weary from it."

"That's strange."

"No. That's just badly made tea."

Slocum returned to Banjo's tent to get more bottles.

"Run out already?" Banjo asked. "Good thing Evan thought better than to stay in town. Figured it was so deserted, we'd be needing some more wash. I don't know where he gets his brains from. Surely not from me, and not from his ma, neither! She ain't got the sense of, er, a hungry hare."

Evan replaced Slocum as house bartender, a job as eagerly accepted as it was relinquished. Slocum wanted to keep an eye on the pair Denahee had pointed out.

"Recognize them two with the black hats, behind the fiddler?"

Banjo strained his eyes. "Ain't seen 'em before," he said. "But I seen their like. Don't suppose they relatives either, eh?"

"Reckon these miners are so swipsey, they look perty easy pickins to a couple murderers like those two."

"Better tell McBean. Iffin this was my place, I'd give 'em the heave-ho, but this is his stretch of wood, and it is his weddin', eh? Knowin' McBean, er, ya know, they might truly be relatives."

Slocum didn't relish returning to the house, but he followed Banjo's instructions next time he went to bring more bottles in.

He found McBean at a huge banquet table, sitting with Denahee, Betcham, Schmidt, Florence, and some bridesmaids, and Duncan, nodding off and flanked by Matthew and Elk Dog. Angelica, at the far end of the table, was gesturing to Evan to fill up the Indians' wineglasses. Florence gave Slocum her sauciest leer.

"McBean," Slocum said, after taking him aside. "There are two bandits outside sizing up your guests. Baines wanted me to make sure they weren't invited before sending them on their way."

"Bandits?" McBean asked, stroking his beard. He glared at Slocum, and went for the door. "I'll see to them."

Mamie came in with a couple tureens of fish soup. Angelica cried out to her, holding up an oblong fritter. "Mamie, what the hell are you serving me at my wedding?"

"Looks like one of them Chinese egg rolls," she answered, winking at Slocum.

Slocum followed McBean out of the house, but couldn't get through the crowds quickly enough to hear what he said to the bandits. They turned away immediately, got on their horses, and rode off on the path going away from town.

"Guess they weren't so tough, after all," Slocum remarked.

McBean sneered at Slocum as though aiming to pick a fight.

"Where's that path lead to?" Slocum asked, looking up at McBean impassively. He was stalling, trying to figure out what McBean was thinking. He was acting distracted and mysterious.

"The canyons, Snake River." McBean had nothing to say to Slocum and bellowed out to the crowd, "Venison and grouse ready for the eating out back. Go for it!" The men whooped and shot off their pistols.

Things quieted down some after the men had eaten, though the musicians kept playing under the full moon. Four bonfires blazed on the meadow, and as the overfed men grew tired, many wobbled close to one of the fires and passed out on the uncovered ground.

When the sit-down meal inside was over, Evan returned to the tent. At his side came Florence. She was not all that pretty, Slocum observed. But she did have some of the biggest breasts he'd seen working west of the Missouri. Her distinctive curvature seemed wasted on a small town like Snake Gulch. There were so few women anyway that the tiniest of nubbins would have been met with enthusiasm.

"Slocum," she said, "you disappoint me." Her gaze went straight through him, bringing a flush to his cheeks. Banjo pretended to busy himself, but well within earshot.

"Angelica said you'd be coming round," Flo continued. "But I reckon that Mamie hussy's been taking care of your needs."

"Please don't speak badly of Mamie," Slocum said in defense of his landlady's reputation. He added quickly, "Fact is, I've been kept busy working for Banjo. I was meaning to come pay the ladies in your house a visit."

Florence turned on Banjo. "Shame on you," she said. "Keeping this fine example of male pulchritude from the lonely ladies of Snake Gulch. You can handle this tent yourself, Banjo Baines, you fat old buffalo."

Banjo was surprised and somewhat insulted. He'd never seen Flo so worked up before. But it was true. Now that it was dark, most of the miners were about as saturated as they could get. And Evan was on hand to help, in any case. "Er, take him, Flo, iffin you're so heated up. Though, you know, iffin this war yer tent, you'd be takin' a commission offa yer employee. Heh, heh."

He'd meant it as a joke, but Flo screwed up her face, dug down deep into her petticoats, and produced a handful of gold coins. "There!" she exclaimed. "It's like Angelica says: gold makes men available, too."

Slocum was pretty popular with the ladies—even working ones like Flo had fallen for his sculpted upper arms—but they always fell after sex, never before. And they never paid. "Hey, what's going on?" he asked. "And, don't I get a say in this transaction?"

Florence sensed she was getting out of line and quickly changed her tack. "Just escort me back to town," she said. "I don't fancy waiting for the others."

Slocum shrugged. He felt he was being toyed with, but he couldn't say why. As he followed Florence down the path to town, he half expected the bandits to attack from ambush.

The buxom blonde rode very quickly, leaving Slocum to pick out the unfamiliar path at a pace the roan was reluctant to maintain. By the time he reached town, without incident, he sensed he'd been more hurried away from McBean's than hurried toward anything.

They tied up their horses at the stable, and Florence led the way to Mamie's, Slocum in tow. He thought she might deposit him there and be on her way. She hadn't exchanged more than a few words with him as they walked down the street.

Then, suddenly, upon reaching Mamie's, she began giggling and waxed loquacious.

She chattered on about her dream of accumulating enough capital in the mining towns to open the most opulent gambling and pleasure palace ever to grace the Barbary Coast. She rattled off an extensive list of furniture she intended to fit her palace with, not sparing details of upholstery or her preference of manufacturer.

Slocum let her do the talking as he took her to his room and freed her bosom from the ties of her laced girdle. The skin of her breasts was translucent, and tender as two newborn porpoises. He slid inside her loins without disturbing her monologue, like a canoe riding white water.

3

It had indeed been far too long since he'd had a woman—at least a week. Satisfied though he'd been at the end of round one, he woke up after just a couple of hours ready to have another go at that blonde madam. He reached across the bedclothes and grabbed hold of an armful of nothing but disappointment. Florence had flown the coop. No doubt she had business to attend to at her own place.

Throwing open the windows, Slocum greeted the bracing morning air with almost as much pleasure as he would have welcomed another dip in the pool of love. Stripped of clothes, he let the breeze wash over his body. It was still quite dark, but even so, it was late enough for the early risers of Snake Gulch to be starting their day. This Slocum knew full well from his late hours at the saloon. After closing time, there was the briefest moment of silence before life started anew.

The moment passed and still the streets were silent.

Downstairs, Slocum found Mamie lighting the stoves for breakfast.

"Mighty quiet this morning," he said. Mamie glared back with her black eyes. She picked up a heavy iron skillet.

Slocum backed away. Looked like Mamie had gotten up on the wrong side of her bed. Maybe she'd seen Flo slip out of his room. Mamie hadn't said anything about lady visitors not being allowed, but she hadn't laid down the law against pig-killing in her boarding rooms, either. These were just things you got to know she wouldn't tolerate too well.

"Reckon Fat Sang can bring me my breakfast to my room," Slocum said, figuring he'd keep out of Mamie's way.

"I sent him round McBean's to fix coffee up for the men who'd stayed up there last night."

"That's nice of you, Mamie."

"It'll be on McBean's bill, nice or not." She glared at him again. Like he was some varmint that might go away on its own, without her resorting to drastic measures. "Reckon you might get yourself a cup up thataways."

Slocum didn't feel tired enough to go back to sleep, so he dressed properly and went over to the stable. Perhaps he could coax a mug of coffee from Matthew and Elk Dog while closing the deal on the Ghost Horse.

The stable was deserted. Slocum bridled the blue-roan, try-ing to shrug off his misgivings. The stable hands, and Duncan too, were always up and dressed by now. Duncan hadn't been well the night before and could have spent the night at McBean's, but Elk Dog would be back minding the ani-mals if all were well. As he rode to McBean's, Slocum felt a tightening in his stomach. Something was wrong and the black-haired horse would endure any punishment rather than hurry along to McBean's.

On the path before McBean's house, Slocum spotted Evan and Fat Sang huddling behind a mule. The roan was ambling along as Evan peeked over the mule to see who was coming. "Slocum!" he cried with relief. "Slocum!" he cried in despair. "They killed Mr. Duncan. The Injuns did."

He halted beside the boys, taking in their appearance, but he didn't linger. The boys were unharmed, just shivering in fright, he thought, swinging off the roan and bounding across the yard to the house. Why would any Indians have killed Duncan? he wondered. How had they gotten to him with Matthew and Elk Dog watching over him?

"Hang 'em red devils by their toes," McBean raged from a

room in the back. "Get a rope and hang 'em. Get 'em devils out of my home and hang 'em!" And the miners echoed his words.

Slocum's heart sank as he entered the house and saw the corpses of Matthew and Elk Dog. The miners dragged them before his eyes, from the hallway to the front room.

"Hold on there," Slocum said with disgust. "Those boys look perty dead to me. No point hangin' them now, is there?"

Blacky finally saw his chance and called out, "The stranger's right. I reckon we might as well hang him in their stead. He's a lowdown Injun-lover if there ever was one."

"You try that, Blacky, and I won't be coming after you with just a whiskey glass." Slocum planted his feet apart and shifted his gaze over the miners. They snickered a bit. Though Blacky was well feared, he wasn't feared enough to be well liked.

Blacky kicked Elk Dog's body and smashed in his face, grinding with the heel of his boot. "McBean says we hang 'em by their toes, and that's just what we're fixin' to do. Anyone puts hisself in our way gets the same as they. Right, men?"

The miners agreed a bit halfheartedly, waiting to see what Slocum would do, their hangovers catching up with them in Slocum's sobering presence.

Slocum stood his ground. "I've talked to Matthew about buying some horses," he said steadily, "and he struck me as being a right Christian man. He had kind words for Mr. Duncan. I have a hard time believing he'd do the old man any harm.

"Even if he was a devil, as you say, Blacky, why didn't he and Elk Dog do their dirty deed to Duncan on the way out here from town, or at any other time? Why take the chance here, when they could've easily gotten away with the crime? No, I'd say they were trying to protect Mr. Duncan."

The miners quieted down, listening in confusion.

McBean came into the room, blood trickling down his forehead from where he'd ripped out a patch of hair to prove to his men his anguish over Duncan's death.

"And now," Slocum continued, "someone's killed these Indians. Killed them without a trial. Killed them without clear-minded people examining the facts to make sure of their guilt. Who would be so faultless, so sure of themselves to judge these boys so quickly?"

"I killed them Injuns," McBean said, challenging the crowd as though he could do the same to everyone else, and no one could stop him. "I killed them heathens that murdered Mr. Duncan."

"You may think they murdered Mr. Duncan," Slocum said, trying to reason with McBean, for the men's sake, "but how do you know they weren't set up? They had nothing to gain by murdering Mr. Duncan."

"What do you know?" McBean bellowed. "Them Injuns want us off this land they claim as theirs. Men, hang 'em devils. Hang 'em by their toes!"

"What's the point of hanging dead men, McBean? A man doesn't go stirring up unnecessary trouble with the Indians, and I'm not convinced they did it. Let's investigate this further . . ."

"The point, Slocum, is to teach them Injuns not to go murdering us white folks." McBean's words were dripping with sarcasm, as though he were talking to some tenderfoot. It played with the miners.

Slocum didn't want to see the Indians' bodies desecrated further. He held up his palms, his body language communicating compassion. "It's a heinous crime, I agree, McBean. But let's not lose our heads. It's a serious business parceling out justice to the Indians on their own land. It's not just a matter of this community, here. There are repercussions affecting all the people of this territory."

"Them Injuns can't be killing us white folks." McBean looked like he was on the verge of exploding.

Denahee, the architect, stepped out, holding the bloody Bowie knife that had eviscerated Duncan. "This knife was still in one of their hands when we found them. No doubt wickedness overtook them after they'd drunk too much liquor."

"Duncan's heart was in the other devil's paw," a miner cried out.

Slocum appealed to Denahee. "That might be evidence of their guilt, I grant you. Still it may be a setup. Let's look into this matter closely. If we find conclusive evidence, I'll take the bodies to the marshal in Lewiston. He'll confront the Nez Percé chiefs, with the law and the muscle of the cavalry behind him."

McBean snorted. "I say an eye for an eye—and worse!" he declared, raising his fist.

Denahee reached up his arm toward McBean's fist. "Restraint, Mr. McBean," he said. "We must exert restraint, though we are maddened by these foul deeds and thus tempted to rampage like the savages. Mr. Duncan's last work was to place you in charge of the men. He meant you to lead them in an honorable way, to show the men restraint by your own example."

"There's a time for action, too." McBean broke free of Denahee's orbit and plunged into the crowd of miners. "We must show them savages, them heathens, what they'll get if they lay one finger on any of us. Hangin' them red devils by their toes—right, men? Hangin' 'em is the only way to show 'em. Tell me if I'm right."

The miners charged the corpses, shrieking and kicking them as if they might get away. Slocum saw that the battle was lost. He watched Denahee, Betcham, and Schmidt retreat to the rooms in the back. He couldn't count on the college boys. He walked out of the house and eyed his roan with disgust. If only the horse had moved faster, he felt, all this might have ended differently. If only he had gotten to McBean's before the Indians had been shot. Even so, he might have failed to save them from their fate.

Slocum glanced over to the boys cowering behind their mule at the path. He tried to mask his defeat as he walked over to them and remounted. "Come on, boys," he said. "I'll go with you back to town."

Fat Sang held back. "Fat Sang collect money for food," he said.

The boy was quite reasonably afraid for his life, but still he thought of his duties. Slocum reflected bitterly that when white folk's blood was spilled, all people of differing races were wisest to lie low.

Slocum rubbed his stubbly chin. Fat Sang was a skinny kid, without a gun or any other defense to give a murderous lynch mob a moment's pause. "You reckon this is the best time for collecting bills?" he asked, nodding back over to the house, where continued bloodthirsty cries indicated the men's spleens were still unspent.

"Mamie say don't return without gold. Fat Sang ask Mrs. McBean. She give gold to Fat Sang."

"Under the circumstances, I think Mamie would understand you coming back empty-handed." Slocum looked at Fat Sang. He was going in, no matter what. "Yep," Slocum continued, "I reckon I'd like to see how the hostess is bearing up under these tragic events. Evan, you coming to collect your pa's bill, too?"

Evan looked up, startled, but the question required no answer.

"Seeing how my cut's coming out of Banjo's payment, I wouldn't mind having accounts settled," Slocum continued. "Can't say when a man might reckon it's time to tip his hat and bid farewell to Snake Gulch."

Evan was afraid, more afraid than he'd ever been. He was inclined to make his way home by himself, and that was scary enough. Slocum grinned at him, hewing off a chaw of tobacco. Evan realized it wasn't enough to follow Slocum and Fat Sang simply because they offered him no other option. It wasn't enough, but it was all he could do.

Slocum led the trio to the side door that opened onto the kitchen. The sounds in the house clearly terrified the boys, but they mastered their trembling as they followed Slocum to the honeymooners' room.

Without even bothering to knock, Slocum confidently ushered the boys into the room. Mrs. McBean lay dry-eyed and stretched out on her bed in her scarlet dress. The one with the hubs. Sweeping off his hat and resting it over his chest, Slocum spoke rapidly. "Excuse me, ma'am. I hope you'll give refuge to these two boys. It's mighty dangerous out there."

She peered at Slocum and the boys with smudges under her eyes. Prominent on the table beside her was a bottle of laudanum.

Slocum pressed on. "You must know how deeply grieved we are about Mr. Duncan. Mrs. McBean, we all share the same tremendous grief."

Her eyes darkened further, but she managed to mumble, "We are grieving. Some can grieve in public, some must grieve in private. I care to . . ." Before she could dismiss them, Slocum finished her sentence for her, to a different end.

"I know ma'am," he said. "You care to know why these boys are out here so early in the morning." Slocum turned toward Fat Sang.

The Chinese boy looked down at the floor, yet he took his cue and spoke clearly and deliberately. "Mamie write out your bill." He held it out. Angelica glared at the boy's slip of paper.

Slocum handed her the bill with Mamie's itemizations and then gave Evan a gentle nudge forward.

"Paw'd like his bill taken care of, too, I reckon," Evan blurted out. "Though ya know Paw—don't expect he'd write out a bill or nothing."

Angelica looked annoyed, but also befuddled. She managed to raise herself up rather regally and glide over to her cedar chest. She gave the boys each a heavy bag of gold, adding, sourly, "This will more than cover your expenses. Weigh it out if you want . . . at home, so I can get some rest, now."

The boys backed off toward the door, and Slocum swept his hat back on his head.

"Wait, delivery boy." Angelica spoke acidly, tossing a smaller bag of gold at Slocum. "I hear you did a fine job last night. Keep that. And stick around town. I'd like to use you again."

Slocum's cheeks burned as he held the bag of gold. "Don't

worry," he said, "money this easy would make most any man available—if all he's asked to do is tote some firewater."

"Just remember to make yourself available when I want you." Her eyes took on a wide, demonic intensity that sent Evan into a panicky gasping for air.

Slocum laughed. "I'm not on anyone's payroll, Mrs. McBean. I'm strictly my own man. Misunderstood you before, thinking you meant this as payment for last night's bartending." He tossed the pouch of gold onto Angelica's bed. "The boys and I will leave you alone now, so you can grieve in private."

Slocum was disturbed, thinking of how Florence might have been a decoy to keep him off the scent of trouble. Was Angelica implying that he could be bought? he wondered, as he turned to leave.

Blacky stepped in the room, one hand thrusting out his Smith & Wesson and the other hand stroking its ridged steel barrel. "Slocum, it's downright rude to turn a pretty lady down. That's something you'll want to be reconsidering."

Slocum ignored Blacky's gun. "It's hard to turn a perty lady down and then again, it's hard for a man to be beholden to anybody." He spoke with a level voice that betrayed no emotion besides an unyielding resolution and growing impatience.

Blacky continued rubbing his pistol, and laughed. "For treating a lady like that, I could blow you to kingdom come, Injun lover. I don't reckon nobody'd care one hoot."

Slocum took a chance. "Seem a shame to heap yet more bloodshed upon this woman's home. A new wife in her new home, having all this blood to clean up after. Must be hard for her."

Angelica, who'd been observing matters with cool detachment, couldn't restrain a mock sob. "Oh, bloodshed in my home," she sniffed.

Blacky didn't get the sarcasm. There's nothing like a bad woman to make a fool of a bad man. Blacky was moved and lowered his gun, saying, "You're not worth the killing nohows. Mrs. McBean here won't be needin' you, Injun lover. Best leave town right quick while you can. By the way, Injun lover, that deed you come all this way to deliver was cut in half by them Injuns you love so much. They didn't like our claim to work their land. They cut it in half along with Duncan hisself. Ha! I reckon you're the delivery boy of useless deeds."

Now Slocum had his Colt aimed straight at Blacky's face. Blacky started to raise his own revolver, but Slocum nodded to the floor and Blacky dropped it fast. Slocum had looked at him with no remorse, like he'd seen him look at Banjo's rats right before shooting them dead in the saloon.

Slipping Blacky's gun into his belt, Slocum tipped his hat to Angelica and led the boys out of the room. "Reckon you'll have to do without your pistol, Blacky," he said, then added in a whisper, "Got to hand it to you, though, you are a lucky man. Before this morning I figured you'd get your just desserts without my needing to help. Now I'm fixin' to change my mind. Can't gun you down in front of the children, though, unless you slip up. Not in cold blood, I can't. I've got to set an example. Slip up and I'll set another example."

Back on the trail leading to town, Slocum rode ahead of the boys, circling off to the sides to scout the perimeters when a meadow opened off the path. The trail was by no means direct, Slocum saw, but wound around the steeper terrain at every occasion. Slocum quizzed the boys about more direct routes to town, and they told him of the path to the house Denahee and Betcham shared, which continued on to town. Fat Sang explained that most everybody avoided that trail because the banker, Betcham, did his trapping in those woods.

At town Evan returned to his father's saloon while Slocum and Fat Sang rode grimly back to Mamie's. Slocum tied the blue-roan to a post and went straight to his room to think.

The Indians had been set up to appear to have killed Duncan. Angelica had gotten them drunk and probably laced Duncan's tea with her laudanum to make him sleep through his murder. With the deed destroyed, McBean and his accomplices were ready to claim ownership of Gold Hill, as it had been foretold McBean would.

As had been foretold . . . It suddenly occurred to Slocum that McBean's next dastardly move might involve circumventing Evan's own promised destiny. It was a wild guess, a horrible thought, and he hoped he was wrong. If the key were Evan, Banjo would mulishly resist seeing his son's danger and would have to be dealt with accordingly.

Hearing a tap at the door, Slocum realized he had been pacing the room. He stopped walking, strapped on his holster, and was about to answer, when the door opened and Mamie entered.

She looked straight into Slocum's eyes with a warmth he hadn't noticed in her before. Her long lips turned upward at the corners. She closed the door behind her gently and said, "Fat Sang told me you helped him get my gold. I wanted to thank you, Slocum."

"He did it himself, no thanks to me. Perty brave kid you have working for you, Mamie. He walked into that house of death as calm and tough as the best grown man I've met." Slocum looked at his landlady curiously, adding, "Doesn't seem like you're much affected by the news of that killing up at McBean's. Not terribly affected for a woman, leastaways."

"You like that, right?" Mamie reproached him. "Frankly, Slocum, I didn't much care for Mr. Duncan. A good businessman, but a bit too rich for my tastes. I'd rather not talk about the boys. They shouldn't have been drinking liquor is all I can say."

"Do I gather that you might think it was not the Indians, but someone else—say, maybe McBean—who killed all three?"

"I'd say that McBean has a lot of friends in Snake Gulch. Besides, why McBean? Why not Blacky? or Donal Denahee? I wouldn't put murder past any white man so long as there's gold involved. Tell me, Mr. Slocum, are you any different? I can see you're a white man, but I can't tell right off if you're the type of white man who's ever profited from another man's death."

Mamie sat on Slocum's bed, arranging her wide skirts. Then she looked up at him and smiled mischievously.

Slocum laughed. "Reckon you have a point."

"That's all right. I've got the white man's blood in me, too, so Lord knows I'm not perfect."

"You're looking perty perfect to me, right now," Slocum countered, sitting close to her on the bed. He wondered what Mamie would look like with her long braid untied, her wild hair over her wide shoulders.

Mamie moved away a short distance. "Slocum, don't be impudent. I'm a lady. I came up here to thank you, not to be seduced by you."

Slocum grinned at her, admiring her plump cheeks, the long stretch of her shiny, even teeth.

Mamie took Slocum's right hand and held it. "I owe you one. Fat Sang is like a son to me, but he's also Chinese and feels his sense of duty beyond all reason. I would never have sent him for the bill if I'd known of the trouble up there. I was very relieved to hear how you stood by him."

"Mamie," Slocum said, releasing her hand, "you'd be helping me out if you'd tell me who I can count on if it ends up McBean's behind all this trouble."

"Someone deputize you, Slocum?" Mamie glanced at him sideways, with narrowing eyelids.

"I'm not the law, ma'am, but I'm partial to justice when it's on my side. Now I don't know this town well, so I'd like help in bringing McBean to justice. The mining officers, the miners, the other people in town . . . Is everyone afraid of McBean?"

Mamie stood, patting down her frock. At length she shook her head. "This ain't your trouble. You best be moving on." She opened the door, stepped into the hallway, and added, "That's my favor to you. It's good advice. Do yourself a favor and take it."

"Thank's," Slocum muttered to her retreating footsteps. He hadn't considered moving on, leaving matters in Snake Gulch to resolve themselves as they would. Now he considered the possibility. Nothing would be easier than to ride off. He could see himself atop the fine silver stallion with plenty of gold tucked away under his vest.

While it was true that he'd get a certain satisfaction from seeing McBean brought to justice, it wouldn't bring back his victims. And though he'd grown to like Matthew, pious and stiff though he was, he didn't feel a pressing need to avenge him. McBean would be a formidable enemy, and Mamie was probably right to advise him to leave the dead to bury the dead.

The only problem was Evan. He was damned if he was about to let any harm come to him from McBean.

Slocum's thoughts were interrupted by a growing noise from the street. A sad, dull ringing of steel axes hewing through pliant pine sounded like so many church bells tolling mournfully. Raising his window, Slocum saw the street lined with merchants cutting planks.

Across the way, the undertaker, a man with salt-and-pepper hair and goatee and a black frock coat, hovered near a younger man hammering away at a coffin. For all his stolid appearance, the undertaker couldn't conceal the glow of avaricious joy emanating from him as he instructed his assistant. It wasn't every day that the richest man in town died.

Miners drifted about the street looking as if they were at a loss for how to act. On the hill the mine was silent. Down the street the barrooms were doing a brisk business.

Slocum rubbed the stubble on his chin and decided to visit the barber he'd gone to earlier in the week over in Chinatown. Although the wizened Chinese man had seemed fluent enough then, as soon as Slocum began asking about McBean, the barber lost his command of the English language.

Slocum interrupted the running patter of Cantonese as he paid his bill. He pointed at a man hard at work cutting a tree trunk half his size into planks. "Why?" Slocum asked.

"Injuns on warpath," the barber said rapidly with fear in his eyes. Clearly, Fat Sang's stouthearted nerves were not representative of the Chinese in Snake Gulch. If he were to take on McBean and his miners, Slocum would find little support among the customers here.

As he walked back to Mamie's, he saw all the merchants laying planks over their windows. Even at Mamie's, Fat Sang and some of the cooks were hard at work repairing the shutters.

In the dining room, Slocum joined a table of men he passed daily in the house but hadn't gotten a chance to know on account of their different schedules. His fellow boarders had no work to do, because the mine was closed, and Slocum seized the opportunity to get to know them better. As he joined their table, they nodded to him in acknowledgment of his greeting, but they didn't stop eating.

When Mamie appeared and came around to Slocum, ladling out a bowl of aromatic venison stew, he said, "See you're shuttering up the place. You also convinced the Indians are fixin' to attack town?"

"Might be," Mamie replied.

"There any Indian braves in the vicinity you know about?"

"None I've seen," Mamie sighed and set down her pot. "Mr. Slocum, I own a business establishment. I have to do what everyone else does, no matter what I think personally. Then again, Slocum," she added sharply, "even if they didn't start it—and we can leave that question unanswered for now—I don't expect any Indians are going to sit still once they hear about them goings-on at McBean's. We are, after all, in Indian territory, and Indians, just like the white man, don't like to hear about their people's dead being treated disrespectfully."

Mamie turned to the miner sitting across from Slocum. "Danny," she said, abruptly changing the subject, "hold on a moment. I don't want you to worry none about this stew meat. Let me cut the pieces up for you."

Danny's right hand was wrapped like a melon, but he clutched his bowl in his left hand, growling. "Don't do me no favors!" He slurped up half the contents of the bowl. The other half of the stew streamed down his chin and soaked the front of his jacket.

Slocum glanced at the man, whose family name he recalled suddenly was Treleaven. The man whose fingers Blacky had shot off. Injured as he was, he could perhaps be of some help. Taciturn by nature, no doubt an obdurate loner like so many of these old-timer miners, and now unemployable in his vocation, Treleaven was one miner Slocum might win over to help nail McBean.

After Mamie had left the room, Slocum bit off a crust of bread and asked casually, "What's your take on Mr. Duncan's murder?"

A long silence followed as Treleaven appeared to think over the question. Finally he turned his head to look at Slocum. "Who the hell are you?" he asked.

A tough egg, Slocum thought, but decided to pursue the subject. "John Slocum. Been tending bar at Banjo's." The miner grunted. Slocum continued, "Doesn't make much sense, them Indian boys killing Duncan."

"I don't think much about who other people kill."

The three young miners at the table grumbled something noncommittal, pushed their bowls away, and stood, not wanting to hear more. Treleaven and Slocum were left alone at their table.

"Heard this theory 'bout McBean—and maybe his pal Blacky—having something to do with them murders."

At the mention of Blacky's name, Treleaven's expression resembled that of a man lifting a heavy load, or one whose nose hairs were being plucked out. But he seemed not to have heard the substance of Slocum's words. With a grimace and bulging eyes, as though in a trance, the injured miner spat out, "I'm going to kill him."

Mamie returned with another bowl of stew for Treleaven. Barely stifling a reproving look at his stew-splattered shirt, she gently scolded. "Danny, you stay away from Blacky. You promised me that much when I mended your hand. Don't you go letting me down again."

Again Treleaven said, "I'm going to kill him."

Slocum almost regretted not having earlier done him the

favor. As a rule Slocum preferred to let God and the courts do the dirty work of judging and punishing. But in this godless and lawless town, a man had to exercise considerable resolve to keep blood off his hands.

Treleaven's remaining fingers quivered in Mamie's linen bandages. He hid the stumpy fist inside his jacket Napoleon-style and rose from the bench.

"Hold off, Danny," Mamie cried, hands at her hips. "You can't take on Blacky with just your left hand. Sit back down and eat!"

Treleaven waddled over to the front door, opened it a crack, and drew his gun.

Mamie held her hand over her mouth and watched silently. Slocum came over to her side, behind Treleaven, as he took his time aiming. The shot blew away the toes from the boot on the shoemaker's shingle. Of course, no man was about to give him that kind of opportunity to aim. Probably not even the careless Blacky, Slocum thought. Still, Treleaven could be useful. He didn't seem intimidated by McBean and his gang.

Mamie put her hand on Treleaven's sloping shoulder. "You still have an eye," she said. "In time, that hand will be as good as the other was."

Treleaven walked out the door without a word in return.

"Makes me feel like I'm fattening up livestock for slaughter, them miners." Mamie sounded a bit sorrowful, picking up the untouched bowl of cut-up stew she'd prepared for Treleaven. Although she didn't add anything else, there was a pleading look to her eyes.

"I don't baby-sit grown men," Slocum said. "Ain't there any law in this town?"

"Duncan was the law and he never troubled himself with bloodshed in the barrooms and squabbles over poker. His motto was a man who dallies with the devil pays that piper and the sooner the better."

Slocum sighed and went to his room to fetch more ammunition.

Outside, whinnying plaintively, Slocum's roan reminded

him he still had much to do. He went down, untied the horse, and led her to the stable for a feed. There he discovered the Ghost Horse missing. A boy of Evan's age was idling in one of the stalls, chewing a blade of straw.

Slocum greeted the boy. "Afternoon. You keeping an eye on the stable?"

"That's right. For Paw, who keeps the general store. Martinson's General Store."

"You know what's become of that wild silver stallion?" Slocum asked, pointing toward the largest stall, where the stallion had reigned.

"Nope," the boy said, spitting out his straw onto the dirty floor. "You must be the gunman Evan Baines keeps boasting about knowing. You that gunman?"

Slocum watered the roan and laughed, brushing aside the boy's question. He peeked out to the corral. The Ghost Horse wasn't there.

"That water's gonna cost you, mister," the boy said, mischievously. "That's right. You give me a dollar for that water."

"*You* are Evan's friend?" Slocum asked, strapping a feed bag around the roan's neck and patting her down.

"I've got a name, too. Clint, Clint Martinson, and my paw runs the dry goods store. Them oats is gonna cost you another dollar. You just gimme that dollar. That's right."

"Put it on my tab, kid," Slocum said, reminding himself that even a snot-nosed kid was still just a kid. He brushed the blue-roan, and when she'd eaten her fill, Slocum retightened the saddle, adjusted the bridle, and took her for a ride about the woods around Snake Gulch.

At first, the mare behaved with docile obedience. Slocum found the waterfall, but no sign of the Indian sisters he'd heard so much about. What had they said? The end was near. Whose end, he now wondered. Elk Dog and Matthew's? Were the Indians really going to attack?

Strangely, in the woods about the waterfall, he could find no recent trace of the sisters, even though the ground, moistened by the rains and snow, was ideal for tracking. Surely the sisters would have left tracks. Had they gone away? Could they be hiding deep in one of the caves?

Slocum declined to explore them. If they were in the caves, he wouldn't disturb them. Heading back to town, the roan rebelliously ground her nose to graze the scrub and veered to the side. Reteaching the horse who was boss took up most of Slocum's energy, and he gave up hope of finding an Indian camp, if there indeed was one. Instead, he applied his complete attention to disciplining her. In the end she brought him back to town with painful obedience, as though she were being made to walk on broken glass.

Back at the stable, Clint looked on as Slocum removed the saddle, examined the mare's hooves, and watered her in her stall. No doubt the boy was about to ask for another dollar, but Slocum silenced him with one steely glance. It was getting dark and he had things to do.

On his way to Martinson's General Store, though, where he hoped to learn what had become of the Ghost Horse, Slocum's attention was drawn to Banjo's Saloon. A passel of shifty miners rode up to the post, Blacky numbering prominently among them. Blacky shot Slocum a look of fearsome hatred as he went through the batwings.

It didn't seem possible that anyone would blatantly murder the boy on his father's own turf. Blacky, however, was deranged enough not to be trusted. Anarchy was carrying the day. Slocum quickly followed the miners into the saloon.

As the batwings closed behind him, Slocum sighted the potential threats. The saloon was nearly full, and Blacky sat at a table with his back against the wall. Yet his hands were easily in view and he hadn't bothered to notice Slocum walk in behind him. Slocum counted to ten and still Blacky hadn't noticed him. Treleaven would have been able to get his man had he had the good fortune to be there just then. Another piece of luck for Blacky, Slocum reflected.

That mustachioed miner and the other men at his table were setting up to play a game of poker, anteing up and shuffling two decks of cards.

On the other side of Slocum, two tables of men had registered his presence, but their alertness suggested a more defensive tack. Of those men, Slocum figured he'd have to keep an eye on just the one called Tubbs, a heavyset black man with a shiny pate. His fingers tapped restlessly on the rim of his whiskey glass and his pistol was riding up his holster as though it were aching to see some action.

Keeping Tubbs and Blacky always in at least his peripheral sight, Slocum edged up to the bar and motioned Banjo over.

"Mighty early fer you, John, eh?" Banjo said, pouring him out a shot. "Ain't it a pity 'bout Mr. Duncan? Reg'lar saint he was. Town won't never be the same again. Lordy, that's what comes from trustin' them Injuns, eh?"

"Banjo, there's some serious business we need to discuss," Slocum said in a low voice. "Been thinkin' hard about McBean, and reckon your boy Evan is in a heap of danger. Where's the boy now?"

Another man signaled for Banjo down the bar. "Er, hold that thought, John," Banjo said. "Let me take care of this customer first. Ye ain't feelin' like gettin' behind the bar a bit early today, are ye?" Slocum shook his head impatiently.

More and more thirsty miners with time weighing heavy on their hands kept coming through the batwings, and no one was leaving. Banjo was getting wound up, miners calling to him from all sides. Alternately he'd be boasting about how much McBean had paid him for the wedding party and then saying what a shame it was Duncan had been killed. When he finally made his way back to Slocum to fill up his glass, Slocum learned that Evan was writing a letter to his mother in his room upstairs.

At Blacky's table the poker game was proceeding mirthfully. The itchy-fingered bald man had joined the game and drawn Blacky's attention to Slocum, just as Banjo was handing him a pouch of gold as payment for the week's work.

Blacky grinned at Slocum, showing off the black pit of his almost toothless mouth under the thick mustache. It was a good thing Blacky didn't grin too often. His interest quickly returned to his hand of cards, though. It appeared he was on a roll.

Slocum was about to slip upstairs when Blacky called out to one of the men standing at the bar, one of Slocum's fellow boarders at Mamie's. "Pick," Blacky cried, "you come on over here. I'm aimin' to win some of your gold."

"Not on your life, Blacky," Pick replied. "You know I can't read them playing cards. Can't read nothing, especially not your playing cards."

Blacky laughed. "Cain't read numbers? You are one ignorant son of a bitch!"

Slocum overheard Pick say to the man beside him, "Even if I could read, it'd save me a sack of gold to play the fool and say I can't. Blacky's deck is mighty partial to him."

The other miner murmured that maybe it was time to head on out, before he, too, was summoned over.

Slocum debated whether it'd be better to take on Blacky now than to wait for him to try and hurt Evan. Sooner or later he'd be sending Blacky to his eternal reward, so it might as well be now.

Just then Treleaven burst through the batwings, gnashing his teeth and crying out, "I'm going to get my gold back from you, Blacky. You're going to do that much for me."

Slocum waited. With his back covered by Banjo, Slocum watched Blacky and Tubbs, ready to intervene when either one made a move. His own arms were relaxed, at his sides. In his mind Blacky was a dead man already. Tubbs he wasn't so sure about. All of Slocum's senses were at full alertness. He was chewing on the tension in the air, savoring it.

Then the lights went out.

4

Banjo and Evan were back on the winding path to McBean's. The chilly air was dark under the completely overcast sky. Dancing flames from the torch Banjo held made the forest shadows twitch like souls tortured in the lower rings of Hell.

Though Evan was indeed afraid of returning to McBean's, his fear was nothing compared to his anger at his father. Why had he struck Slocum? he wondered. How could he side with Blacky? Evan was disconsolate.

"I expect McBean has a plan laid out fer you, son," Banjo gossiped cheerfully, oblivious of his son's unhappiness. "Now, I don't want you to go agreeing with the first thing he offers, mind you. Jes thank him, er, polite-like, like your ma's taught you. Eh? Then I'll do the talkin'. It'll be a hardship on me, I do reckon, after all, when you're not 'bout the bar to help out. Eh? I jes know he's got somethin' special fer you—and I won't be the one gonner hold you back, son. It's in the stars: one day you'll inherit the mine. First, I reckon, you've gotta learn them ropes. Can't be countin' on knowin' your trade till you learn it—remember that. You're sure gonner end up better'n me. I reckon it's too late fer an ol' dog like me to aim at improvin' our lowly station, such as it is. So it's up to you. Er, and you do good, perhaps we can go fetchin' your ma back home."

Banjo was only increasing his son's animosity toward him. Evan stopped listening and let his father prattle on, the words passing mistily over him, tingling his skin without sinking in.

Evan couldn't escape the image of Slocum slumped to the floor, Banjo over him still brandishing the club. This is what he had seen when he ran from his room after Treleaven's plaintive cry about his lost gold.

Evan was reluctant to question his father about why he had hit Slocum. He didn't want to be ashamed further; he wished the episode could disappear from his memory. Yet he couldn't help thinking his father a coward, kowtowing to Blacky to keep on McBean's good side. Then, to Evan's amazement, Banjo began boasting of his shameful cowardliness.

"That Slocum turned out to be a real troublemaker, eh?" he was saying. "An Injun-lovin' troublemaker. Lucky I whacked him in time. Could've been another bloody mess. Maybe you could mention that to McBean iffin you can slip it in. Er, a man shouldn't have ta brag about his own deeds."

"He was just standing up for Danny Treleaven," Evan complained meekly.

"Ol' Danny can't take of hisself, eh? Reckon that's true, fer he ain't good fer much without them three right-handed fingers. What business had he comin' after Blacky where he can't defend hisself? Blacky's no good as a man, but he's a fairly good customer, I'd figure. Most prob'bly brings in a goodlier number of customers than he, er, takes away."

"Before yesterday, you're always wishin' someone would put Blacky down," Evan said less meekly, more bitterly. "Mr. Slocum would've smoked Blacky if you hadn't clubbed him from behind."

"With men like Blacky, you respect their power or you're not long fer this world," Banjo chided.

"At least Treleaven and Slocum didn't grovel at Blacky's feet like you."

"Blacky came especial to me with a message from McBean, sayin' we gonner talk 'bout findin' you a job in the mine. You're a sensible boy—you don't think McBean would've taken kindly to us if I'd let Slocum smoke Blacky, eh?"

"See! You're a coward!" Evan cried out, and for the first time in his life, he looked at his father with undisguised hate.

Banjo gulped and stopped walking, his son's words reddening his face like a slap. To add to the humiliation, a gust of cold air blew his hat and toupee from his head. As he bent to reach for them, he heard the sound of hooves cantering around the spur in the woods beyond the path. Banjo threw down his torch and grabbed Evan tightly, pulling the struggling boy down to the ground. The father's strength prevailed, and they crouched and huddled together.

Two men on horses appeared on the ridge, pointing shotguns at father and son. Banjo recognized them as the bandits from McBean's wedding. He stood up, out in front of Evan, shielding him, with his hands raised. "I'm unarmed," Banjo said, reading his death in their eyes. "Quick!" he cried, turning and pushing Evan toward the woods. "Run away! Get goin', son. Now!"

As a shotgun blast ripped into his father, Evan ran for his life into the dark woods.

The moon was full behind the ceiling of clouds. Evan ran in the iridescent forest as snowflakes enfolded him. He ran in speechless terror, sweat leaking from his skin, burning in the cold night. He couldn't understand that his father was dying. He couldn't bear the thought. He ran toward the darkness of Betcham's Wood, always toward the blackest stretch of night. As the horses pursued him he thought only of the shameful things he'd said to his father.

He ran and imagined his tread so light that Betcham's snares were sprung beneath his winged feet. His legs sprang up too fast to be caught, too fast to be glimpsed by the murdering bandits, the men who'd killed his pa.

Slocum imagined millions of tawny butterflies licking the sweat from his body and dancing on his eyelashes. He opened an eye and the butterfly loomed large, white and crystalline before him. He blinked, and the vision melted into a drop of water.

Snowflakes swirled about him as he lay, he realized, crumpled over himself in Pissmud Lane. The Colt was gone, of course, as well as his gold. And the Stetson from Mary Jane in Kansas City. Slocum picked himself up off the ground, his anger conquering the nausea and dizziness from the blow to his head. He'd been buffaloed by Banjo—that much was clear.

A deathly silence enshrouded the saloon. Slocum brushed the mud from his leggings and noticed that the window to the mining office was ajar. In there, he thought, would be a decent map of the area. Something he could use, since the residents were so ignorant and/or hostile. Nobody had been either able or willing to tell him anything about the land surrounding the Gulch. He hoisted himself through the window, only once inside realizing how exposed and chilled he had been.

He fumbled through his pockets for a Lucifer. Fortunately his robbers had left him his cigarillos. He fired one up and lit a lamp. He tried to collect his thoughts, come up with a plan. He felt wildly impetuous. He wanted to join forces with the Indian camp and attack the Gulch, retrieve his gold. He wanted someone to come find him snooping about the mining office. A face-to-face battle was always a welcome tonic after being whacked from behind.

He nevertheless moved about the room quickly and kept the lamp shielded from the front windows. The German geologist, Schmidt, had his desk in the corner, apart from the other tables in the room. Here Slocum located mineral tables and sheaves of paper abounding with scribblings about chemical compounds.

Slocum sifted through the papers, scanning each in the time it took to turn the page. There were a few maps and many reports detailing the soil composition at various sites in Snake Gulch. One site was where the banker Betcham and the architect Denahee shared a house, midway between town and

McBean's, on the parallel trail to the one Slocum was now familiar with.

Denahee had spoken about restraint. He and Betcham hadn't seemed in collusion with McBean, but would they be of any help to him? Slocum wondered.

On Duncan's desk Slocum found a packet of correspondence from the marshal in Lewiston concerning the supply road Duncan was building. Passage down the mountainside was going to be accessible to wagons or at least ox carts. Apparently right now all supplies came via pack mule. Clarkson's tone was cautioning, but he never specifically wrote anything about this road being a further invasion on Indian lands. Surely there had to be Indians nearby if the whole town was in a frenzy over them. But where were they?

Slocum hoped to find out how badly the Indians were taking the news of Matthew and Elk Dog's murders. He realized he wasn't about to join their cause directly, but perhaps he could head off a direct confrontation between the townsfolk and the Indians. He didn't want the situation to get any messier. It would be hard enough to get back his things without bloody mayhem breaking out all around.

As for Evan, Slocum couldn't bring himself to think about that. Banjo and Evan had gone off someplace, leaving him for dead, or at least unconscious and in an unspeakably filthy alley. No, Slocum was not going to think about Evan right now. Peace between the Indians and the townsfolk was an easier objective. What would make him feel better, he knew, would be to retrieve all his personal belongings and ride away on that silver stallion. His mind was reeling. He sat down and examined his feelings to get a grip on himself. He was going in too many directions, and the reason, he suspected, was his anxiety for Evan's safety. But so far he hadn't a clue where Evan was.

Before leaving the office, Slocum riffled through the notebooks on McBean's desk. McBean's predecessor, Fletcher, had personnel records that amounted to a register of most all the town's inhabitants over the past three years. Duncan had begun working the claim with Denahee and Betcham in his employ. It appeared that Fletcher and Schmidt had arrived together, summoned from the East by Duncan once he'd proven his claim had enormous potential.

That was mildly interesting, but Slocum was more impressed by the number of Indians who'd worked initially at the mine. The names were crossed through, indicating they were gone now. And after the initial page of Indians, the log listed only the usual mining names, of Welsh and Cornish origin. Where were the Indians now?

It was time to see Martinson. Slocum stepped out of the mining office into a gusting flurry of snow that was covering the town. His jacket was warm enough, and his anger kept his face and hands from feeling the sting of the cold. Martinson's was midway to Mamie's on the main street. The storekeeper was locking the door to his shop when Slocum got to it.

The man looked like his son—small, dull eyes set far apart, a round nose with enlarged nostrils.

Slocum expected Martinson to be able to answer at least one of his questions, although by now he didn't expect much from the residents of Snake Gulch. The shopkeeper only let Slocum inside because he pushed his way in the door. Over the counter was a sign: "WE BY YOUSD CLOSE & PISSTALLS."

Martinson was not immediately forthcoming with the information Slocum was seeking. He didn't know where Banjo and his son had gone. It was news to him that the saloon was closed. The merchant believed that the barman had gotten rather too grand of late, ascending to the heights of Snake Gulch society merely by holding onto McBean's coattails, as he saw it.

Martinson had a much better stock of whiskey, but that wily Banjo had gotten to McBean first and sewed up that wedding deal with his rotgut. It was shameful, he said. Maybe Banjo was at his still, making his week-old grain whiskey.

As for the Ghost Horse, Martinson said he didn't want to speculate about who'd stolen that prize animal, but, he said, "Ah couldn't put it past that wily Banjo Baines." Whispering, he added, "And thar be Injuns in them woods."

"Where exactly in the woods are they?" Slocum asked.

Martinson shrugged. Slocum stared at the storekeeper, waiting for him to start getting down to a closer semblance of the truth. The storekeeper wasn't easily intimidated. Instead he went on the attack.

"My boy Clint say you've a horse with us," he said. "Best you settle your bill and find yourself another stable 'fore them thar Injuns steal your horseflesh. Ah can't look after the store and the stable at the same time."

Slocum reached inside his shirt as though going for his pouch and then lifted his empty hands to Martinson. It was an ambiguous gesture, but the merchant smirked sadistically. "Course if you ain't got the boardin' fee, ah reckon ah can figure out some work you can do for me."

Slocum was not about to work for anyone in Snake Gulch again. "Don't worry 'bout my horse's upkeep," he said. "You'll get your payment when I get fixin' to leave."

"Ah ain't guaranteeing them thar Injuns won't come sneakin' in and steal that thar nag of yours. And then Ah will be out what you owe me for its upkeep. Say you best leave that holster you got thar, so Ah know you won't run out on me. Ah see you don't got no gun for it, anyhows."

"I don't need a gun," Slocum drawled, cracking his knuckles.

Martinson dropped his eyes.

"Now, I want some real answers," Slocum said. "First, where's Banjo and his son?"

The merchant hemmed and hawed till Slocum placed his hand firmly down on the other's flabby shoulder. Martinson's expression resembled that of a butt-headed cow about to be tipped.

"They say that thar Evan of his war going to get a job in the mine. That Evan of his is always abiding by his daddy. Not like my good-for-nothing Clint. Evan's a runty boy, no good for mine work. But did McBean want Clint, a big, healthy lad better suited for mine work? Only reason not is because Banjo

Baines has got him wrapped around his fingers. Him and that thar whore and Banjo and his son, they went up to McBean's to talk about the boy's new job. That's all Ah know. Ah think you can take your hand from my shoulder now . . ."

Slocum left it where it was. "By the way," he said, "where're you keeping that wild stallion?"

A gaunt woman in a gingham cotton dress descended the staircase in the back of the store and walked out into the light, her Winchester aimed at Slocum's crotch.

"Mrs. Martinson, I presume?" Slocum said. "How do you do, ma'am."

"I know all about you, Mr. Slocum, you Injun lover. And I heard what you said to my husband in that high and mighty tone of yours. Now, I was you, I'd take off that holster and set it on the floor and take yourself and your fidgetty old mare out of town 'fore mornin'. Bad-talkin' McBean."

Slocum quickly thought back to whom he had shared his suspicions of McBean with. Looked like Treleaven had been talking with Martinson. "I'd tip my hat to you, ma'am," he said. "Except someone seems to have borrowed it for the moment. Only for the moment, I assure you. Nobody would have tried to sell it to you, would they?" He swung around the door, adding, "I'll be taking my horse now and you'll get your payment; I'll make sure of it."

He kept the holster, and stopped by Mamie's to get Blacky's pistol to fill it.

Bathed by the heavy snow, Slocum rode through the low-hanging storm clouds along the mountain path to McBean's. Having already traversed the path the night before, he made his way easily through the flurry. He thought of that ride behind Florence, of his premonition that violence was in the air. How much had she known? he wondered. Slocum tried to dismiss his suspicion of conspiracy. Although he had been sorely disappointed and abused by the people of the Gulch, it didn't follow that they were all working in concert.

The path was a smooth sea of snow, obliterating the tracks of the others who had earlier gone ahead. Yet at one spot he sensed that something was out of place and drew up on the reins. It wasn't the telltale sign of a struggle that stopped him. It wasn't a strange sound, exactly. It was the quiet the hunter hears after fatally surprising his quarry.

He explored the area briefly—the trees around the spur—but found nothing. The snow had masked the scene of the crime. The body, about to exhale its final thin breath, was further obscured by a rotten log.

It didn't take long for Slocum to reach McBean's. He tethered the roan off the path a short distance behind the house. There were three miners guarding the house: two by the front door and one at the back. A small fire burned off to the side of the front of the house, where the bodies of the Indian stable hands hung by their feet.

Slocum went to the rear of the house and lobbed an iceball at the eaves so a shower of packed snow fell upon the guard. The miner looked up, imagining that the snow had been thrown over the house.

"Pick," the guard cried, "I've had enough of your horsin' 'bout." He stomped off over to the guards at the front, allowing Slocum to dash over to the windows looking into the dining room.

"I did not throw no snowball," he heard Pick cry out. "Musta fallen from the roof, you fool. Put that snow down. Come on . . ."

On the far right side of the dining-room table, McBean lorded over the gathering. The blond mining officers, Betcham and Denahee, sat facing the window, and Slocum could only see the backs of Angelica and Schmidt's heads. Blacky was relegated to the far left end, separated from the group by several empty seats, and Florence leaned up against his side like a lovesick pigeon.

They hardly looked to be a coven of conspirators. Each person seemed to inhabit his own world, so divergent were the expressions on their faces. Mamie stood by the door with her arms crossed as Fat Sang served her dishes. She looked the most distressed.

Slocum cracked up the window to hear the conversation.

McBean was asking for another plate of camas.

"Right away, Mr. McBean," Mamie said, her voice resonating with the cold chime of a cashbox. Those camas would cost plenty.

McBean was flushed, either in high spirits or high on spirits. His booming voice was twice its normal volume as he resumed regaling the mining officers with tales of his former campaigns against the red man.

"This last time," he was saying, "I got wind of the travails of a wagon train just half an hour too late. Saddest thing I ever did see: This darlin' wisp of a girl-child with toothpick arms was dangling from her pappy's broken wagon, her bloody frock torn . . . up over her head."

"The savages!" Denahee exclaimed, pounding his fist down against the table. He then blushed, embarrassed at his outburst.

McBean chortled. Mamie unfolded her arms and stamped from the room, Fat Sang at her heels.

Slocum hadn't been able to see much of Angelica, just her black hair twisted and piled up on top of her head, the taut nerves in her long, pale neck. Now she showed Slocum her profile while turning to smirk at her husband, a private exchange. She and McBean held themselves regally. Their lips were identically stretched in firm lines across their faces.

Though sinister, they were still far more attractive and appealing to the eye than Florence and Blacky at the other end of the table. Blacky belched in Florence's face, and she returned the compliment and then toyed with his mustache.

There was a tension among the others, who seemed to be waiting for something or someone. Slocum wondered if they were waiting for Banjo and Evan. And where were they, anyway?

As if reading his thoughts, McBean cried out, "Banjo!" with surprise. The table turned to look at the door. No one was there.

The color drained from McBean's cheeks as he leapt to his feet. "Banjo," he said, leaning in toward the door. "But what's wrong? Are you hurt? What's this blood? And where's your boy?" McBean looked back at the puzzled guests at the table. "Why won't he speak?"

Angelica tittered, and stepped gracefully around the table, taking McBean's arm under hers. "Oh, McBean, you make us laugh. Oh! Now the air is cleared of that suspense of waiting for him to come. Oh, see?" She pointed toward the window, and Slocum ducked just in time. "The drifts are growing higher. He delayed too long before setting out."

McBean pulled back. "Don't you see him? Standing there . . . bloody, his arms are reaching out . . ." McBean stared at the space beside the door.

"Now the joke grows stale. You men!" Angelica bent her head between Betcham and Denahee and smiled. "I'll never understand why you must run everything to the ground."

"They run everything below the ground, that's why," Blacky quipped.

Angelica laughed heartily. "Now, that's funny." She linked arms with McBean again. "On that merry note and since it's obvious that Mr. Baines is not showing up tonight, I think we should all get some rest."

"Angelica, we haven't etten yet," Blacky objected.

Denahee rose quickly, though, pushing in his chair with finality. "That's an excellent suggestion, Mrs. McBean. We can discuss our strategy for dealing with the Indian hostilities tomorrow, then. And, Mr. McBean, if Mr. Baines isn't interested in your plan to fortify his saloon as our headquarters, we can just as easily use the mining office, as I recommended."

McBean remained distant and troubled, leaving Angelica to fuss after the departing guests. Once they quit the room, McBean muttered to himself, "A ghost. His ghost has come to haunt me. Is this too much for me to bear?"

Slocum listened as the dinner guests, Mamie and her helper, and the miners outside all made their way from the house.

McBean remained at the table as Angelica cleared the dishes, lost in her own thoughts.

Just as Pick rode off on the path toward town, Slocum saw the two bandits emerge from the path from the canyons. He pressed against the building as they rode to the post. Slocum peered around the corner as they rapped on the door.

Angelica greeted them with silence and closed the door on their faces. A moment later McBean stepped out. "How did it go?" he asked gruffly.

"We got the man. The boy escaped."

"He is dead then. I see." McBean rubbed his beard.

"You have our gold?"

McBean dug into his pockets and pulled out two bags. "Two punches," he said. "And what about the boy?"

"He's in the woods, Betcham's Wood."

"I'll keep one pouch for later, then."

The bandits took the other pouch of gold and rode down the path toward Betcham's Wood. McBean looked after them, muttering, "This won't do." He left the door open as he pounded through the house, grabbed his coat, and returned outside. The storm had passed and the clouds were thinning.

Slocum gave McBean a good lead on the path through Betcham's Wood. McBean's tracks were the heaviest and the bandits kept to the sides. All were easy to make out in the eerie moonlight.

When the path rounded the Denahee-Betcham spread, the tracks divided. The bandits had ridden toward town and McBean toward the falls. The trail to the falls quickly became steep, dangerously slippery from the snow and ice. The blue-roan was more stubborn than ever, and finally she would not budge. Slocum dismounted and led her protesting all the way to the high ground above the foaming cataract.

He tied her a distance from McBean's black stallion, and made his way down a rough footpath. Because of the deafening crash of the falls, he almost overtook McBean, as the giant miner stopped to load his Winchesters. At length, McBean turned onto a footpath leading straight into the spray.

Slocum followed along. Past the spray, the ledge widened gradually into a cave carved into the black rock. The mouth of the cave looked out upon an arc of white water swirling in the cold moonlight. As his eyes adjusted, Slocum saw a small fire in the rear of the cave casting enormous shadows on the back walls. He held back at the side as the Indian women began singing. They sang about the great birds and mimicked their calls.

"Stop that infernal racket," McBean said and silenced them. He shouldered one of his rifles. "Now, I want some straight answers to some simple questions."

"McBean is here," one voice cackled.

"Our time is over," another continued.

"Brown bear sleep. Awake in hunger. The end is near. Rising is far. Hard, hungry, and far."

"No more riddles," McBean ordered. "You said that Baines boy is going to inherit my mine. Tell me when. Tell me what I can do to prevent that. Tell me and I'll reward you."

"Stay away from Slocum!" one of the women shrieked.

Slocum figured that was pretty good advice. He wondered if they had spotted him. He crouched down, but he couldn't figure out how they could have seen him. All he could see of them was the fantastic shadows that loomed up the rear wall. He was also surprised by how clearly he could hear them, considering the roar of the falls. Acoustics were strange in caves, he figured, magnifying some sounds and muffling others. In fact, he thought he had heard the familiar whinny of his roan.

"Yes, I've had my eye on him. You're right about him. Tell me more. Tell me about the boy."

"We are many. The people will return when the buffalo return. You are one."

"The great one!" another woman cried out.

"No man of woman born will harm you!" cried the third.

Slocum had heard that one before. It didn't include babies taken out from cesarean sections.

"You say I'll die a natural death? No man will kill me? Hmm. But tell me about Evan Baines."

"The end is near. You are the one. The great one! You have the day. Not till Betcham's Wood flies before your eyes will you die, McBean."

"Another riddle . . . or are you saying I ain't gonna die? I sometimes think it is possible, for some, to avoid that fate we're taught to expect. Who's to say there are no exceptions? I've seen strange things I wouldn't have believed and heard great tales. The world is full of unexpected things, surprises."

Slocum thought he heard a sound behind him, and as he turned a shot rang out. Now there were just two shadows on the wall. He rose, drawing Blacky's Smith & Wesson. "Your game's up, McBean," he yelled out.

The other rifle discharged in his direction. Slocum sprinted to the rear of the cave, where McBean was attempting to reload.

"Just drop it, or you're going to die a hell of a lot sooner than you think."

"Slocum, you pestering me about killing some squaw?" McBean set the rifles down.

"Just step aside of those Winchesters. I'm taking you to Lewiston, where you'll get a fair trial and a fair hanging."

"I don't reckon the courts want to squander their precious time looking into our Injun trouble up here in the Gulch. This is war, Slocum."

"Shut up and get to the side."

McBean started laughing and Slocum felt a heavy blow to his head. He rolled away, seeing Schmidt coming after him, kicking the Smith & Wesson from his hand and kicking his body closer to the edge of the cave. He looked up at the barrel of McBean's Winchester and just managed to push out of the cave, down into the thundering water, as McBean's rifle discharged.

5

It was a drop of thirty feet from the cave to the deep pool of foaming, freezing water. Slocum was a good diver and a strong swimmer, but it was sheer luck that saved him from the pounding water of the falls and the treacherous eddies. Quickly spinning his arms, he scooped himself out of the pool and collapsed over a boulder at the edge of the water just in time to hear two shots ring out from the cave above.

Idly he thought of Blacky's pistol. He had left it in the cave after Schmidt kicked it from his hands. Now, as he lay on the banks of the pool, gasping for air and shivering, he was overwhelmed with regret that Blacky would be strutting about town tomorrow with his pistol. And Slocum resented that all he would have to show for himself was his own empty holster.

He raised himself up a little off the boulder, but immediately sank down again. He had to get up. The air was cold, and he couldn't control the shakes that racked his body.

From above a familiar, terrified whinnying helped Slocum come back to his senses. He saw, at the head of the falls, his black-haired roan thrashing in the water, fighting against the inexorable currents—that pulled her over the edge.

That did it.

Slocum rose, waving his fist in the air, yelling into the roar of the falls, "Damn you, McBean!"

Despite a multitude of aches in his joints and muscles, he made his way back to the cave. As he dried off in front of the fire he contemplated the bodies of the old Indian women. Unlike their looming shadows, they were incredibly small and bent, almost hunchbacks.

He brushed away the wild manes of white hair from their faces and closed their eyes. Their skin was lined with countless wrinkles and covered with moles from which long steely whiskers had sprouted. They wore ill-fitting untanned elk hides that exposed their breasts—and the bloody wounds to their hearts.

It might have made sense to spend the night in the relative safety of the cave, but Slocum didn't feel comfortable about sharing the space with the corpses. In any case, the fire was dying out and there was no dry wood about to pile on top of it. Although he could have easily collected some wet branches from outside, the cave would then have filled with smoke. It looked as though the Indian sisters had figured they wouldn't be needing the fire much longer than they did.

Slocum wondered if the sisters had been planning to go off and join their people elsewhere. They had no food with them, no beads or belongings, either. Perhaps Banjo had been right: Maybe they had come to the cave to die.

It took an hour for Slocum to return to Mamie's. Fat Sang let him in, reporting that everyone else was asleep. Slocum was confident that no one would be looking for him there. Presumably between McBean and Schmidt, anyone else wanting to do him harm would by now have been told of his demise at the falls.

Slocum slept deeply, but he hardly awoke renewed and refreshed. Instead, he was only marginally better than paralyzed with pain when he opened his eyes. As he lay on top of the bed, moving various bones just to make sure they weren't broken, he listened to the household sounds. With the clattering of pots and pans and the loud footfalls, there was also an urgency of movement that was unusual, a constant coming and going through the front doors and hushed whisperings.

By the time Slocum had loosened up his aching muscles enough to sit up, Mamie was at his door.

"So you aren't dead," she observed, looking down at him, hands on her wide hips.

Slocum couldn't tell if she was disappointed. He tried to stand, but his legs were still too unsteady. Mamie grabbed ahold of him before he toppled over.

"They found that horse of yours dead at the falls. What happened? You ride over the falls last night? Hmm. Look at that bruise." She helped him lie back over the bed.

"The horse and I went over separately." Slocum winced with pain and with the horrible memory of the hapless roan in her fall to death.

"I don't think I want to know about it." Mamie paced the room, glancing furtively out the window. At last she added, "Slocum, I don't generally go telling people their own business, but if I was you, I'd get out of town real quick."

Slocum made another attempt at standing, this time by leaning on the wall. That way he could work on his legs, leaving his back for later.

"I know it's none of my business," she continued. "But in my line of work I hear things, and people are saying you're spying for the Indians. I'm not saying it's true. And I know it ain't. But it's what the people think. And they're not feeling kindly about it, especially not now that Banjo and his Evan have gone missing. People are looking for someone to take their anger out on."

"Bring me something to eat, Mamie."

She was about to add something else, but decided not to. "Right away, Slocum," she said without emotion, leaving the room.

Slocum felt bad about that. She was just trying to be helpful, after all. He didn't have to be cool with her.

When she returned with his plate, Slocum grabbed her

and pulled her into his arms. He kissed her with a hungry passion.

She broke free and pushed him away. "Are you mad?" she cried, wiping her lips with her sleeve.

"If I'm doomed to get gunned down by the fearful citizens of the Gulch, I figure I might as well die with a smile on my face. Don't you like me, Mamie?"

"I don't think you understand the danger you're in, Slocum."

"The danger can wait. Come over here, Mamie."

"Slocum, the danger is right outside. McBean's talking to the men in the shantytown. Pack up and leave right now. You may not get another chance."

"First off, I have nothing to pack up. They've taken my gun, my horse, my hat, and my gold. All I got is some time, which I'd like to use up with you. Come on, lie down beside me."

"They took your gold?" Mamie screwed up her eyes.

"See. I've got to stick around if you want me to pay for breakfast."

"Who took your gold?" Mamie's foot was tapping impatiently.

Slocum managed to wrap his arms around Mamie's ample waist. He whispered in her ear, "Stop talkin'." He pressed her close to him.

She whispered back, "Who took your gold?"

"I can't rightly say. I was buffaloed by Banjo when I turned my back on him last night at the saloon. You'd think I'd know better than to trust anyone in a mining town." He nibbled at her neck. She brushed him away.

"Oh, shush your mouth. Who else was in the saloon? Was Danny there?" Slocum murmured an assent, reaching out to untie Mamie's braid. She stepped back. "Why, he took it. I knew something was fishy when he said Blacky had paid him back for the poker game. That scoundrel. And it's all my fault! I asked you to look after him. Well, don't you worry none. I'll get it back for you."

And out the door she went, leaving Slocum feeling damn silly. He wouldn't let a lady fight his battles. As quickly as he could, he pulled on his boots and was down the stairs after her.

All the miners boarding at Mamie's were seated around the table. Slocum noticed that Treleaven and Pick tried not to look at him.

"Blacky didn't give you that gold, did he?" Mamie was saying to Treleaven.

The three young miners tried to stand.

"Sit back down," Mamie ordered. "No one's leaving here till I settle this." Slocum opened his mouth to take charge. She silenced his with a severe wagging of a finger. "You. You stay out of this," she ordered. "I asked Mr. Slocum to look after you, Danny . . . Is that how you repay me the favor? Haven't you any decency? Did any of you have mothers or were you all raised in a wolf pack? You, Pick, look at me."

Pick's eyes skulked about the corners of the room before finally being drawn to meet Mamie's stern gaze.

"I know you were at Banjo's last night. You tell me what happened."

"Ask Treleaven," Pick squawked. "He took the money."

"Okay," Mamie said, holding out her palm. "Hand it over," she commanded Treleaven. "Hand it over or out you go. I've looked after you in your misfortune like the mother that bore you. You cross me now, you'll regret it the rest of your dismal days."

Treleaven looked about the table sheepishly. One of the pimply young miners murmured, "Give it up. Don't mess with Mamie."

Treleaven produced the bag of gold. "I got only one of 'em bags. You gonna get Blacky to give back the other?" he demanded gruffly.

Mamie snatched the pouch. "Blacky's not my concern," she snapped. Turning to Slocum, she added haughtily, "I'll keep this for you, since you can't seem to keep hold of your belongings."

The men around the table snickered. Though it hurt Slocum to see Treleaven getting a smirk in at his expense, he figured he'd have to take his lickings from Mamie with the rest of them.

"Sit down," she said to Slocum. Then she instructed Fat Sang, who was always in attendance it seemed, to bring them all more food and plenty of coffee.

It was a bit awkward at first. Everyone wished he was somewhere else. Mamie was seriously interested in maintaining the peace, however, so the miners grudgingly remained where they were.

"Now, boys," she warned, "I don't want no talk about Injuns or Injun lovers. I don't want no trouble under my roof. Don't try me. We can all get along. I'm counting on you to keep the peace today on the occasion of Mr. Duncan's funeral. You men thought highly of Mr. Duncan, right?"

"He was a fair boss," one of the miners ventured.

"Never did nobody no harm, I reckon," another said.

"I don't like to talk bad about the dead," Pick ventured, "but I hear McBean's gonna give us a fairer wage."

The miners pounded the table with approval. Mamie shot Slocum a meaningful glance.

"Someone, who I ain't namin'," Pick continued, glancing at Slocum, "is claimin' that our McBean did Mr. Duncan in. The rest of us figure it was them you-know-who's and their friends."

"I don't want to hear any more speculation at this table," Mamie stated, "or there will be no dessert. Let's not dwell on controversy. Let's contemplate the good that Mr. Duncan brought us on this day of his funeral. He developed Gold Hill and provided us a livelihood. He deserves to be remembered with thanks."

The miners lowered their heads automatically, as though offering a silent prayer. Mamie smiled at Slocum. Under the table she placed her hand over his. And after a moment, she further admonished the men. "I'm counting on you to spread the word that today is to be a day reserved for remembrance and mourning. Any man who comes here for Sunday dinner, after the funeral, better behave himself. I don't want no controversy in my house today. Now, you go spread the word in the shantytown, and when you come back, I'll have some pies made up special for you."

Some of the miners grumbled that they didn't know anyone to tell, but with one glower Mamie sent them all out the door with her message to spread through the Gulch.

"Well?" she said to Slocum with expectation, still holding onto his hand.

"Later," Slocum answered, patting the hand. "Right now, I need a horse."

Mamie lowered her eyelids, embarrassed, but trying not to show it. "I was asking you how you liked the way I handled them. What d'you need a horse for?" she asked, suspicious.

"It's time I paid a visit to Betcham and Denahee."

"Take my horse," Mamie offered crisply. "It's in the shed out back. Fat Sang will get it for you and tell you how to get there." She sighed and held out the pouch of gold.

"You better hold onto that for me," Slocum said. They exchanged flickering smiles.

Slocum felt a trifle disloyal to the memory of the roan, so smooth was the ride Mamie's gelding gave him. The poor roan might indeed have had some intimation of the disaster awaiting her in Snake Gulch, but if so, she should have also had enough sense to realize that making life difficult for Slocum wasn't about to change her fate. Better if she had behaved more nobly; then at least she would have been remembered more fondly.

Betcham and Denahee were at home, washing up their breakfast dishes, when Slocum arrived. They were both blondish men in their twenties, tall with thin faces. Betcham was the leaner of the two and the more muscular. Denahee wore wire-rim spectacles, which conferred upon him an aura of intelligence. Neither looked pleased to see Slocum. They didn't look startled, though, so Slocum assumed they hadn't heard of the incident at the cave.

"Gentlemen," Slocum began. "I'm aimin' to take McBean to the law in Lewiston, and I figured I should let you know beforehand why. Looks like he's got your partner Schmidt in league with him, by the way. And they're up to no good."

"This is outrageous," Denahee objected. "McBean's of no concern to the law."

"That horse I've been riding about town was lent to me by the marshal at Lewiston. McBean and Schmidt pushed her over the falls last night. If that don't concern the law, I'd be most surprised."

"You see them push your horse? I bet it was them Injuns," Betcham said, setting his jaw to the side.

"Impossible. McBean had already shot all the Indians in the vicinity."

Denahee's mouth was open, silently gasping, "Oh!"

"This business has nothing to do with us," Betcham quickly put in, looking at Denahee with narrowing eyes, trying to stop him from talking.

Slocum picked up on the look. "Denahee, you're an educated man," he said. "I reckon you've already begun to suspect McBean of killing Duncan, haven't you?"

Denahee nodded. "It's horrible to imagine."

"It's Mr. Darwin's law of nature in the wild," Betcham said, again preempting Denahee from committing himself to an opinion. "Might makes right. If you wish to prove yourself the fittest, you go ahead, Mr. Slocum. You and McBean fight it out, but don't go dragging us into it."

Denahee stood, raising up his hands to silence Betcham. "William!" he cried. "I cannot let Mr. Slocum think us craven, cowardly men. Clearly we can trust him. He has come from the authorities in Lewiston, after all."

Betcham held his tongue.

Denahee turned to Slocum. "Mr. McBean has been acting

very odd of late," he said. "Last night he acted as if he had lost his mind. We took Mr. Schmidt into our confidence, sharing our fears, and when he argued in favor of Mr. McBean, we let him think he had us convinced. But we were not taken in. We've drawn up a plan . . ."

Now Betcham leapt to his feet. "Enough!" he yelled. "Do you have to tell him everything? Let him tell you what his plan is . . . how he's going to politely ask McBean to come take a ride with him to Lewiston so the law can hang him for killing the marshal's mare."

"I can handle McBean," Slocum said flatly. "I'm just making sure nobody gets the notion to run off with the bank, Mr. Betcham, thinking that there's no one interested in law and order."

Denahee and Betcham sank back into their seats. Betcham shook his head incredulously, but didn't come up with any response.

"I'll level with you men," Slocum continued. "McBean's got a lot of support with the miners. He's tapped into the townspeople's fear of an Indian attack. They look to McBean to defend them, and they're not going to like me taking him away. But they also look up to you two as officers of the mine. McBean has been doing his best to discredit me, so my warnings to the people are falling on deaf ears."

"Perhaps we can be more visible in town," Denahee suggested. "Show the people we're willing to take control."

"I wouldn't mind moving into Duncan's house," Betcham remarked.

"William," Denahee said, exasperated. "This is serious."

"I'm serious."

"Speaking of Duncan," Slocum said. "I think I'll be getting on to his funeral. It's going to be starting shortly."

"We're the pallbearers," Denahee said sadly. "We should all go together. McBean won't try anything at the funeral if you're with us. Likewise, we shouldn't test the miners' respect for us by bringing up the issue of his crimes just yet." Denahee left the room to get his coat.

Slocum turned to Betcham. "Why is it, do you think, that the miners respect you?" he asked. "Is it on account of your money?"

Betcham flinched and dug his hands deep into his pockets.

The three men followed one another to the town square. Because the church was merely an ash heap and a pile of timber, the funeral service was to be held inside Duncan's house. Few of the miners and merchants had been inside the opulent white mansion, so the mood of the mourners going into the house was more of eager curiosity than sorrow.

High on their horses Betcham sneered at the townspeople and Denahee sat rigidly, trying to command respect. Slocum kept his eye fixed on the stable.

There the pasty-faced Clint Martinson was, with wild gestures, relating something to McBean, who nodded, reached down from his horse, and patted the boy on the back, sending him running down a back alley. McBean summoned one of the miners to replace the boy and oversee the stable.

Slocum and McBean locked eyes as the three men approached the stable. McBean was distracted, however, and while registering a trace of bewilderment, it seemed he had more important matters on his mind.

"Greetings, Mr. Betcham, Mr. Denahee. I'll meet you in a short while over by the funeral parlor," McBean said. Turning toward Slocum, he muttered, "The men aren't feeling too kindly toward the friend of the murderers of Mr. Duncan. On this day of his tribute, I'd keep a low profile if I was you. Been doing my best to keep Blacky from coming after you, for example, but in his state, I wouldn't turn my back on him."

A group of passing miners stopped to spit in Slocum's direction, and only then did McBean discard his tentative tone toward Slocum. It was as though he wasn't certain Slocum was real till others responded to him. "Watch yourself."

"You're something else, talking about Blacky when it's you who's pulling all the strings," Slocum retorted. "Pulling the strings, that is, when you're not actually pulling the trigger."

"You're a stranger here, Slocum, and you've got your facts all screwed up. But ignorance ain't gonna excuse you." The miners started coming toward Slocum. "No," McBean told them. "Keep on walking, boys. Let's show our respect for the great founder of our town by holding off till after the funeral." At that, McBean rode off in the direction of the mine.

"Where's he going?" Denahee asked, sighing with evident relief. Slocum shrugged, thinking of perhaps following.

"Probably gone to get the preacher," Betcham suggested.

The men handed over their horses at the stable and the two mining officers went to the funeral parlor. Slocum followed the crowd into Duncan's house.

The ground floor was composed of three huge rooms brightened by crystal chandeliers and filled with sturdy oak furniture standing on legs carved into grotesqueries. The overstuffed sofas and leather divans were already occupied by the heavyset matrons of the Gulch, wives of the town merchants, Slocum assumed. One corpulent battle-ax held her spindley husband to her side as she gossiped loudly.

A hand reached out to Slocum. It was Mamie, wearing a becoming black bonnet. "These people are such vultures," she whispered. "Just look at the bulges in those ladies' skirts. Paperweights, carved boxes, decanters even. Did McBean see you?"

Slocum nodded. "He's planning something right now I got the feeling. He rode over toward the mine. You got a notion why?"

"Sure. It's nothing. There's a bar nearby the ravine, called Mercury Drinks. It's not uncommon to find some mining chemicals in the bottom of your shot glass there. It's that sort of low place, but our minister, Mr. Laboite, frequents the joint. McBean musta gone to get him. He's a bit of a . . . well, you saw him at the wedding. Disgraceful, really."

"I still have this feeling McBean's up to something. Would he be able to get Laboite to say I killed Duncan, for example? And if so, would the people here listen to him?"

"I don't think so. Everybody here was raised with religion,

but the people are not too keen on the stuff. Laboite has no sway in our community. Not least since the whole story about him got out, when his Evangelical Church of the Redeemed Spirit burned down. That story being that he started out as a missionary priest in Wyoming Territory but switched churches because of complaints about his womanizing with the Shoshones. And, incredibly, he has a record of setting fire to his congregations. Liquor and candles don't mix. Now hardly anybody'll give him any help rebuilding . . . but he won't leave town. These days he sermonizes 'at the well,' as he says, giving out 'amber baptism' to whoever will buy him a drink. Don't worry about him. He's a joke."

At that moment Laboite appeared at the door, sober, dressed magnificently in his white alb, and swinging a smoking censer in front of him. Following him, the casket was held aloft by Denahee, Betcham, Schmidt, and three other grim-faced pallbearers.

"Maybe he's turned over a new leaf," Mamie whispered.

If Laboite hadn't been at Mercury Drinks, who had McBean been rushing off to? Slocum wondered.

The pallbearers were followed by Angelica and a throng of black-clad mourners, with Blacky's band and Florence's girls taking up the rear. Many of the miners stayed outside, having failed to wash up well enough to look respectable. Right as the door was being closed, McBean arrived, perspiration soaking the front of his shirt.

With the new arrivals there was no breathing space in the house. McBean took his position at the front of the room, beside the other mining officers, and Laboite commenced his recitation.

Slocum thought he heard shots in the distance. "Who's missing?" he asked Mamie, leading her slowly backward into the next room and then the third.

Mamie looked about and then peered out the window at the crowd there. "Baines and his boy and the Martinsons. They all ought to be here."

Slocum pushed back through the crowd to get to the front

door. Laboite was droning on in Latin, so Slocum had everyone's attention. As he opened the door, a wail went up from the miners crowded around the house.

"Fire!" they cried. "The town's on fire!"

Slocum stepped briefly to the side of the house and watched as a good number of the mourners scurried through the door with horrified expressions on their faces. Mamie was one of the first to elbow her way through the crowd. Slocum swept her off to the side.

"Put me down, Slocum. I've got to save my place."

"It's not your place on fire. It's Martinson's. I saw that boy Clint go down this alley. Can we get to the back of Martinson's this way?"

Mamie took his hand and the two ran down the muddy alley. It twisted around shanties and hovels before passing behind the dry goods store, which was blazing on its Main Street side.

Flames had engulfed the front porch of the building, but the back wasn't on fire yet. Slocum tied his bandanna over his nose and mouth to filter the smoke as he kicked the back door open with his boot.

The fire wasn't so bad on the inside. Maybe it was a botched job. Maybe it had been set for the purpose of getting attention, putting a scare on the town. Martinson and his missus had holes blown through their chests. The tomahawk Slocum had given Evan was lodged in Clint's throat.

Looked like the murderers had got the wrong boy.

"Evan," Slocum called out, in case the boy was still hiding in the store. He looked behind the counter. The cashbox was open and empty. Just as he'd suspected, his Colt and Stetson were stashed on one of the shelves. He grabbed a box of shells and then dislodged and reclaimed the tomahawk. He couldn't very well return it to the boy, but he didn't want the Indians to have to shoulder the blame for the murders.

The smoke was filling up the building, though the townspeople seemed to have gotten the fire under control from the outside. Slocum was about to leave when he spotted Evan crouched beside the broom closet by the staircase.

"Evan, you okay, boy?" Slocum asked, kneeling down to him.

The boy's blue eyes gazed up at him with inexpressible sadness, muddy tearstains on both cheeks.

Slocum swept up the boy in his arms and rushed him out of the back door. He quickly surveyed the shacks of the nearby shantytown for rubbernecks, feeling spied upon.

"We've got to hide the boy. Where would be best?" Slocum asked Mamie. "At your place?"

"He won't be a secret long at my place, what with all the miners coming round to eat their Sunday dinner." She screwed up her forehead and looked to the slushy snow on the ground. "He'll be safe at Widow Parkens's. And she'll be home, too. She held a grudge against Duncan."

"Are you okay, boy?" Slocum asked Evan. "Can you walk?"

Mamie caressed his cheek, smearing away the muddy tear tracks. "Where's your papa?" she asked.

Evan pointed to the swirling sky. "In Heaven," he said.

"It's okay, Evan. You stay strong, now. We got to get out of here. First things first. You get down under my skirts, now, you hear? We don't want anyone seeing you, so you stay under my skirts and I'll shuffle over there by the water wagon." She pointed down the alley to the main street, where the smoke was clearing. "When we get by the wagon, you slip out under it. Hear?"

"Who killed the Martinsons?" Slocum asked as Evan crawled under Mamie's skirts. "Was it those two big men with mustaches, the bandits? Have they just been here?"

A muffled "Yes, it was them."

"I'm going lookin' for 'em," Slocum told Mamie. "You'll stay with the boy?" She nodded, her brow wrinkled with concern as Slocum headed through the shanties toward the mine.

The mine was built into the side of a barren hill, separated from the shanties by the tapering end of a gully. The portal was padlocked, so Slocum ambled down the ravine a short distance. The shack called Mercury Drinks was empty, but there were footprints and hoof marks coming and going down the ravine. Slocum recalled from the map he'd seen that the gully curled back around to the Chinatown before veering off into the uninhabited parts of the northern woods.

At the Chinatown, a bridle path went up from the ravine, leading out to the back side of a joss house. Two brown horses, the bandits', were tied to a post. An old man peeked cautiously out the temple doors. Slocum didn't need further proof: The bandits had left their horses and were expected back soon.

Why weren't they back already? Slocum wondered. If they thought their job was done, it wasn't likely that they'd risk getting caught by going to McBean to get their payment. What if they knew Clint was not the boy they needed to kill? What if they were still looking for Evan, and had been hiding nearby when Mamie said she'd take him to the widow's? Slocum broke into a run.

He was unfamiliar with the winding alleys of the shantytown, but he had a strong sense of direction, and was soon back at the main square. He noticed that the water wagon was back beside the stable.

Duncan's funeral had resumed. As Slocum skirted the square, the mining officers followed Laboite from Duncan's house, carrying the coffin toward the graveyard across the street. Slocum continued on to the widow's cottage.

He burst through the door expecting the worst, a bloody struggle with the bandits poised to slice Evan and Mamie's throats. The room was quiet, though. The Widow Parkens sat in an armchair facing him, reading from her Bible. She hadn't flinched.

"Excuse me, ma'am," Slocum said, holstering his pistol. "I was afraid I'd find some bad men stirring up some trouble round here."

The woman raised a black sickle-shaped eyebrow. Slocum remembered she was Angelica's sister. She conveyed the same arrogance. Tall, shapely, and there was a family resemblance in her features—but they had been disfigured by a pox. She looked back to the book on her lap.

"Those whose names are not written in the book of life," she said, "are thrown into the burning lake of sulfur."

Slocum edged into the room. Something was odd about the way the chair was positioned away from any light source.

"I guess you're wondering what I'm doing here, ma'am," Slocum said, as though he were taking off his hat and relaxing. Instead, he approached the widow tentatively, alert for any movement out the windows or in the room. Besides several pieces of heavy furniture capable of concealing a person, there were two doors slightly ajar leading off the parlor. "Please don't be alarmed. I'm a friend. I've come to help."

"You are no friend of mine, mister," the widow said. "I do not make friends with murderers and fornicators. But the time is near when our Lord will set things straight. Let the sinner sin and the unclean remain unclean . . . Do you know your Revelations?"

Slocum didn't appreciate the vengeful gleam in her eye, but he refused to be drawn in by her rancor. He continued scanning for movement and was soon rewarded. Though it was barely perceptible, he spotted the glint of gunmetal at the crack of the second door. In a moment, the Colt was smoking in his fist.

The Widow Parkens screamed and hit the floor as though it had been she who'd been shot. Then a thump, as the gunman behind the door fell to a heap.

"Where's the other one?" Slocum asked the widow, who pursed her lips together stubbornly. "Listen, lady," he said, aiming his Colt at her aquiline nose, "I don't know what your problem is, but these men ain't heralding Judgment Day. They're out gunning for an innocent boy."

The widow covered her ears, but she glanced in the direction of the other door.

Slocum positioned himself against the wall next to that door. It was also opened a crack, but he couldn't hear anyone behind it. He pushed it open further and a fusillade rang out.

The widow's parlor furniture and knickknacks were shot to smithereens.

Slocum peaked around the corner of the door. Inside the room was dark. "What's in here, anyway?" he called back to the widow.

"That's my sleeping room," she answered in a quaking voice.

"Any exits?"

"Just the window, but I've boarded it up."

Slocum considered offering her some comforting words, she sounded so insecure and terrified. Yet, his pity did not overcome his basic antipathy for her. "I suggest you make your way outside," he said. "But keep it low. You wouldn't want to get hit by a ricocheting bullet, Mrs. Parkens."

He watched her crawl all the way to the front door, where she reassumed her proud manner, brushing off sawdust and shards of glass from the folds of her dress.

"Now, what are you planning to do?" she asked, as though it were all his fault.

"Well, don't reckon I know for sure," Slocum said. "Suppose we smoke him out?"

"My husband built this house with his own hands, mister," she said, opening a cabinet near the door and taking from it a musket. "And I aim to protect it."

"You know how to use that?" Slocum asked, wiping his brow.

She raised the musket at Slocum. "As God is my witness," she said, "I shall never be put down again. Get out of my house! Get out, I say!"

"Ma'am," Slocum tried to reason with her, exhaling deeply to keep his composure, "let me handle this my way." He thought about shooting the rifle from her hands, but couldn't bring himself to risk injuring her. Ladies just weren't liable to turn dangerous all of a sudden like this—unless there was a romantic connection. She was just bluffing, and not to be taken seriously. For now, however, he'd humor her, see if he could coax her to be more cooperative. "Okay, how do you want to play it?"

"You in my room," the widow yelled at the bandit. "Don't go messing up my things. You and this gunman best take your battle outside my house. I'm taking him out now. You come along, too. You hear me?"

"That's right," the man answered. "You go on outside."

The widow led Slocum out the door, making a beeline into the woods beyond the path. "He'll be a fool to come out the front door or the parlor windows," she said. "But if he does, I can take him easily from here. You go around the other side. The windows on that side are boarded up secure, but he might pry away the planks. My bet is he'll sneak out the back door. It's five feet from the door to the woodshed."

It sounded to Slocum like a plan, as he took up his position behind a fence in back. Then he noticed the chimney. He'd have to go in the house, after all.

The back door was well oiled, and Slocum slipped into the house without making a sound. He had to move fast, but he didn't want to alert the assassin, either. He came across the body of the one he'd killed in the hallway. Slocum had to drag him away from the door to get into the parlor. A quick look around. The coast was clear. Slocum didn't lose a moment, but strode to the fireplace in three steps and fired up the shaft. At the same time he heard a shot ringing outside.

6

By the time the townspeople figured out where the shots came from, Slocum had moved the widow into the house. She'd only been winged, but it looked like she was losing a lot of blood. The scar wouldn't make her any prettier, yet somehow the injury had transformed her, blown away some of her religious zeal and ill will.

The womenfolk fussed over her, mopping up the blood and arguing over the tourniquet, while Doc Chin, the town sawbones, was sent for. The men prodded the bodies of the bandits and retold the story of the battle, embroidering it as each new group of people arrived to gawk.

Slocum spotted Mamie signaling for him to step outside with her. "What happened?" he asked.

"Evan disappeared, must've slipped away when I wasn't looking. I got him under the water wagon and that's the last I saw of him."

Slocum was perturbed at the unapologetic way Mamie tended to present matters. "I guess it worked out for the best," he said, shrugging. "He wasn't too fond of the widow. You been looking for him?"

"Everywhere," she sighed. "I'm worried. And McBean's been stirring up the people at Duncan's house, saying the Indians killed the Martinsons. The storekeepers are raising a

96

caravan to go up to Lewiston tomorrow."

"Maybe now that they can see the real culprits, they'll calm down," Slocum said. He was uneasy, wondering why McBean would want to perpetuate the myth that Indians were attacking. Was it a setup for more murders to come?

"McBean's convinced the miners, and you can't talk sense to shopkeepers. They trust in whatever everyone around them is buying."

"What about Denahee?"

"He and Betcham were looking disgusted and riding back out to their place last I seen 'em."

"Spread the word that Denahee's thinking about making the trip to Lewiston himself to bring back reinforcements to restore order to the Gulch. Meanwhile, I'll let Denahee in on the news."

"What are we going to do about finding Evan?"

"I'll find the boy."

Mamie accepted Slocum at his word and didn't lose any time, but attached herself immediately to the gossipy battle-ax he'd seen at Duncan's funeral.

Slocum got Mamie's gelding and rode over to the alley around back of Banjo's Saloon, Pissmud Lane. When he was lying in the mud after getting buffaloed by Banjo, Slocum had seen the ground packed smooth in one place where the saloon had been propped up a couple feet. He returned to the spot, dismounted, and crouched on the ground, calling out Evan's name.

After a rustling, the boy peered out from under the building.

"Evan," Slocum said. "How'd you like to go to Lewiston to see your mama?"

The boy's face lit up briefly, but then clouded over. "She don't want me," he said. "No one wants me. I'm trouble."

"You're a brave kid," Slocum said. "And she'd be a fool not to want you. Is your mama a fool?"

"My maw may be a fool," Evan said angrily, "but it ain't fer you to say."

"I don't think she's a fool, Evan." Slocum tried a different approach. "Come on out, boy, and we'll ride out over to Denahee's place. You like Mr. Denahee? You trust him?"

"I don't know."

"Well, we're going to have to trust him. Denahee's going to take you to your mama. At least I'm going to ask him to, and with any luck, he'll be happy to have a reason to leave."

"Really?" Evan was impressed that an important man like Denahee would do him such a huge service. Then he turned sad again. "Why not you, Slocum?"

"I've got a couple accounts need settling. Come on, Evan."

"Can't I stay here? I feel safe here. Nobody but you has ever found me here."

"You can't stay under the house. Your nose will freeze to an icicle and break off."

"But I can't leave my gold. Paw said it was mine. I can't leave it."

"You can take your gold with you. Go on and get it and come along."

"But I can't. It's over yonder, all over the dirt over yonder. It's beautiful, but you can't see it from there. It's right under the floorboards where the miners weigh out their dust."

"You can come back for it," Slocum said. "For now, you'll be better off in Lewiston."

"Are those men still looking for me?"

"No. Don't worry 'bout them."

"D'you kill 'em? That what you mean? You kill 'em, Slocum?"

"They're dead. That's all that matters."

"But it's wrong to kill. You can't go to Heaven if you've got blood on your hands, can you?"

"Don't worry 'bout me. Come on, boy. Get up on the horse. We've got to go."

Evan obeyed, but as Slocum prodded the gelding, he whispered, "I'm afraid. If you're not good enough to go to Heaven, but you're not bad in your heart—what happens when you die?"

As Slocum rode hell-for-leather to Denahee's, he thought over the boy's troubling words. He remembered the tomahawk in Clint Martinson's neck. It was going to be hard on Evan, he realized. He would have liked to have been able to offer allowances Evan would accept, but it was impossible. There was no absolution for murdering your best friend, even in self-defense. Perhaps it was simply the boy's punishment for choosing such a bad friend.

Slocum kept the horse at a gallop, despite the boy's fearful trembling. If the boy were concentrating on staying on the horse, he wouldn't dwell on his recent terrors. At the Denahee-Betcham spread, Slocum maintained his gruff, unyielding demeanor.

Denahee was downing a tumbler of scotch at his table.

"Betcham around?" Slocum asked.

Denahee looked back at him, probing for a hidden meaning to the question.

"I'd just like the both of you around, so I can say my piece one time instead of twice," Slocum explained.

Denahee nodded, reassured, and topped off his tumbler again from the bottle of imported Glenlivet. "Would you care for a drink, Mr. Slocum?" he asked. "It's a small wake, not to be confused with the reign of violence in town."

"Perhaps you'll want to slow down," Slocum observed. "You're going to have to do some hard thinking after what I'm about to tell you."

Denahee set the glass down. "Frankly, Slocum, I am hard at work this very moment trying not to think."

Slocum and Denahee exchanged looks, and Slocum guessed that Denahee had recognized his present predicament, that McBean had taken effective control of the mine himself.

"Well, there's a way to stop him," Slocum drawled, firing up a Havana he'd had the presence of mind to pocket on his way out of Martinson's. "There's the law in Lewiston."

"The law, the law," Denahee said sadly. "Yes, there's always the law. How could I be so stupid? Everything fell apart so fast, and now it's every man for himself."

"It is upsetting." Slocum glanced over at Evan sitting patiently by the window seat. The boy was holding up better than Denahee.

"What can I do, Mr. Slocum? Tell me, what can I do?"

"Go see the law in Lewiston. I know the marshal—you'll like him. He's a good guy."

"You're making fun of me, but perhaps you're right to." He sighed. "No, I can't."

"Where is Betcham?" Slocum demanded, flicking an ash in Denahee's drink.

"Listen, Mr. Slocum. You can't hold me responsible for him."

"We'll hold Betcham responsible for his own actions. In the meantime, you could inform the marshal in Lewiston that McBean hired assassins to kill this boy, though they only managed to kill his father and the family that ran the dry goods store. That will do for starters, at least. Marshal's name is Clarkson. Tell him to bring the cavalry."

"Why does McBean want to kill the boy?"

"He's bad luck for him. I don't know. It doesn't matter. What matters is that someone take him to safety. Are you going to help restore order to the Gulch or not?"

"Of course I shall. I had rather thought you wanted me to . . ." Denahee's words drifted off, and that was the end of the discussion. He gathered up his jacket and followed Slocum, who appropriated and bridled up a horse for Evan.

"I'd better take a gun or something," Denahee said vaguely, right before setting off.

Slocum agreed. "Excellent idea."

"Mmmm, well."

"You don't have a gun?"

"Betcham has some firearms." He didn't move to get them.

"You can't shoot?"

Denahee considered the question for a moment. There was no getting around it. He tried clowning about, exaggerating his drunkenness to hide his embarrassment. He moaned to Evan, "Oh, I'm just helpless, helpless. What about you, kid?"

"Come on man," Slocum said to Denahee. "Sober up." He thrust the tomahawk from inside his jacket out at Evan. "Evan will protect you with his axe. If trouble comes, he'll be able to defend you good as any man. But he can't help you if you fall out of your saddle, so sober up."

Evan beamed—his first smile since Slocum encouraged him to get his payment from Angelica after Duncan was killed. Smiling helped, but still deep inside he felt a raging fear.

Slocum decided it was wisest to accompany them down the rough trail to the supply road. By then Denahee would have sobered up.

It was dark when they reached the road.

"Try and make it to Lewiston tonight," Slocum advised. "Don't stop except to rest the horses." He was confident they'd eluded McBean's grasp.

"You'll wait for us, Slocum, won't you?" Evan asked. "You'll wait for us to come back?"

Slocum watched them ride out into the valley and listened to the night for an hour. Anyone who tried to catch up with them now would have to pass Slocum on his return journey up the mountain. No one did.

Mamie's lamps were dark, but she was only half-asleep, lightly snuffling in the chair by the staircase. Slocum's footfall stirred her to semiconsciousness.

"Slocum," she murmured, rubbing her eyes and getting to her feet. "I left some food warming."

He had been too preoccupied to notice his hunger. Now he followed Mamie to the kitchen nearly delirious from starvation.

Holding up the lid of a huge pot, she peered down into her stew, inhaling the simmering herbs. "*Veau Réchauffé*. It just gets tastier and tastier the longer it cooks," she remarked with self-satisfaction.

Disappointment was written all over Slocum's face.

"What's wrong?" she asked kindly. "Doesn't it smell good to you?" It looked like poor folk's leftovers, but he said with exaggerated sincerity, "When a man's got a hankering for a plain slab of meat, he don't want it Frenchified with a bunch of plants. Guess I'm not sophisticated."

Mamie meant to please, however, and covered up the stew. "I've been tenderizing an especially juicy, thick cut of elk meat for you, matter of fact. I can chicken-fry you up a couple of steaks in ten minutes." Slocum grinned. "Sit down over there at the table and get comfortable," she continued. "How many steaks you got a hankering for?"

"Oh, I don't know," Slocum said, thoroughly enjoying the royal treatment. "Three or four . . . better make it five to keep on the safe side."

"Coming up!" Mamie took a couple pails from under the counter and headed toward the door. "I'm going to boil up some bathwater for you, too. Slocum, you smell like a skunk."

Slocum tried to protest. Just the night before he'd taken a bath of sorts at the falls, after all. He'd gotten wet, at least. "You want me to bathe before I eat?" he complained after Mamie returned from the pump.

"Can't you do two things at the same time?" She smirked, lighting a fire under the water, then adding, "Speaking of skunks, I got news for you about the latest skunk to show his true colors."

"Betcham?"

"Betcham. He's run off with the bank, he has. McBean's taken a posse after him down west to the canyons over by the Snake River."

"Gives us a holiday from McBean for a time."

Mamie then grilled Slocum about what he'd learned from Evan and Denahee. She kept close attention, remaining quiet till Slocum had related everything they had said and implied.

"How long before Denahee leads the cavalry back here to save us?" Mamie was slightly sarcastic and also partly worried-sounding.

"Depends on the weather—looked like a storm was building up down in the valley. Clarkson ain't really his best in bad weather. Tends to keep to his bed if it's wet outside. If we get a blizzard, it could take the soldiers at Fort Lapawi perhaps two days, maybe three, to get here, maybe longer if they're tied up with other matters."

"In other words, we can't count on them at all." Mamie turned to Slocum, looking at him with her earnest bloodhound eyes. "Blacky didn't go with McBean, Slocum. He's been spreading nasty rumors about you and the Indians all about town. The shopkeepers have been coming to me, telling me I should kick you out of your room, and the miners who came round for Sunday dinner were boasting about how they're going to string you up next to Matthew and Elk Dog."

Slocum shrugged. "I'm not worried by Blacky."

"Of course none of them knew that I had my own plans for you," she said, dragging out an unwieldy tin-plated tub from a corner of her kitchen. "Take off your clothes," she demanded.

Slocum hemmed and hawed. "Kinda drafty in here," he complained.

"Slocum, you're not getting shy on me all of a sudden?"

He stripped.

"I hope that tub will be big enough. You're bigger than you looked dressed," she remarked, with a saucy grin. "Take away their clothes, most men look half the man they make themselves out to be. Not you."

Slocum squatted down in the tub. "Nothing I like more than sitting buck naked on a chilled piece of metal."

Mamie countered by pouring almost scalding water over his head.

"Aw!" Slocum cried. "You're burning me like one of your stews, Mamie. Whose side are you on, anyway?"

"I don't know why it is that the tougher the man is and the more caked on the dirt over his body, the more like a baby he becomes when it's time to clean up. You just lean back and stretch out and act like you would if I was carving out a bullet with a rusty blade."

Slocum grit his teeth as Mamie scrubbed over his skin and scalp with a brush that must have been made of porcupine quills. Even her soap was uncommonly abrasive, like a bar of nettles. Given that his body was already bruised and battered from the falls the night before, he did indeed act as though she were performing a painful surgery. He didn't betray the extent of his pain.

At last she was through with the rough scouring, and the final pails of searing water felt pleasant by comparison. Slocum sank down in the water with relief as Mamie got to work frying up his steaks.

"How's Mrs. Parkens holdin' up?" he asked, remembering the sad widow, thinking on the coarse nature of the ladies of Snake Gulch.

"That bandit did her a favor, grazing her arm with his bullet. All she's ever wanted, I'd say, is to have folks feel sorry for her. Now all the wives have moved into her house to hold her hand and hear her tell about fighting off the bandits. She never got that kind of sympathy when her husband got killed, 'cause she blamed it on McBean—and everybody always liked McBean. They just thought she was jealous, 'cause her sister was so pretty and she so plain."

"Did McBean really kill her husband?" Slocum asked, growing drowsy in the warm water.

"Parkens was digging in the mine and his section collapsed on him—it does happen. Another man was killed, too. Thing was, Parkens didn't like Angelica, his wife's sister, working at Florence's. She moved there to get even with Lydia after they had had a blowup fight over money. And while Parkens was waylaying Angelica at every opportunity, trying to get her to leave Florence's, McBean had meantime taken quite a shine to her, and was doing his best to keep her busy at Florence's. One night it was like an auction out there, I heard, with McBean and Parkens bidding higher and higher to spend the evening with Angelica. Parkens outbid McBean, and the next day Parkens was dead."

"No one bothered to look into the mine collapse?"

"The widow handled it like a stupid woman, you ask me. She went straight to Duncan, telling him first off that a miner had killed her husband, 'cause he was trying to save her sister from the whorehouse. Well, Duncan was just not the sort of man who could listen to such things. He tossed her out, saying they all got what they deserved."

Mamie slapped a board on the tub and set a plate of sizzling steaks under Slocum's nose. "I'm not going to have to feed you, am I? You look as tuckered out as the cock that lost the fight. And I've got a heap more scrubbing to do on those feet of yours if I'm going to let you climb under my clean sheets tonight."

As Slocum sliced into his first steak, the juices swelled off the rare meat.

Mamie was as good as her word. After she dried him off, she sent him to the room off the kitchen, a large, feminine bedroom with wallpaper and baskets of dried and perfumed wildflowers.

When she followed him, only a few minutes later, she had untied the long braid that had hung like a thick rope down her back to her waist. Freed, Mamie's hair swung about her upper body, the curls brushing over her nipples as she unbuttoned her dress. There were twenty-odd buttons down the front of her dress, and she unloosened them with tantalizing carelessness.

Her skin was hot and moist, and Slocum popped his load quickly the first go-around. He fell into a deep, dreamless sleep for a couple hours and woke hungering for round two.

Then, after they had screwed like barnyard animals for a considerable time, Mamie got up to make breakfast for the miners.

"Reckon I'd better be getting back to my room," Slocum said, already missing Mamie's down mattress, which was also far superior to his own on account of the promise of a round three to come.

"No, you stay. Nobody's going to think to look for you here, and I've got to warn my borders to keep an ear open for what trouble Blacky's sending our way. Besides, I'd like you to keep my bed warm for me. It's looking mighty cold outside."

And so they spent the morning thrashing about the sheets every few hours. When she wasn't attending to the affairs of her kitchen staff and boarders, Mamie busied herself pleasuring her body and Slocum's, straddling his manhood with her silky thighs.

Slocum was content to lie in bed. The snow was building up outside the window, and he took advantage of Mamie's absences with refortifying naps. When she returned to the bed, she'd bring little cakes and, even sweeter, recipes for amorous delights she'd always wanted to try, but hadn't till now found a man with the necessary attributes.

After a lunchtime interlude, he suggested they pay a visit to the widow. "I'd like to start setting the record straight with people, while McBean's not about intimidating folks. Do you think people will believe me if I tell them I saw him give money to those assassins?"

"No," Mamie said simply.

"Hmm. Guess I'll just have to charm those ladies that you said have moved into the widow's house. If I can get them to mistrust McBean, their husbands will help keep order when the law comes to take him away." Slocum was also hoping to stay the animosity that might fall on Mamie due to her association with him. It was one thing for him to stand up to McBean when the scoundrel was supported and protected by the whole town. But if he could convince them of McBean's guilt, Mamie would also be safer.

"Slocum, nobody's going to believe you if you talk bad about McBean. The storekeepers are all counting on him to catch Betcham and to bring their savings back. And the miners are behind him a hundred percent, no matter what."

"That's why I'm going to start working on the good wives. They might be worrying about their savings, but they're more worried about their families ending up like the Martinsons. And I'm going to tell them it wasn't the Indians who killed the Martinsons."

"Why are you doing this, Slocum? This isn't your trouble."

Slocum thought about the Ghost Horse. He thought about Clarkson coming to the Gulch and finding it in the grips of McBean. "I've still got one pouch of gold missing," he said.

"Okay. But I'm going with you to the widow's. I know these women."

"I don't know, Mamie. I'd rather you didn't get involved. It'd be better for you to look as neutral as you can."

"I can walk over there with you and still look neutral, can't I?"

Of course she couldn't, but there wasn't anything Slocum could do, discounting hitting her over the head, which Slocum had learned from Banjo was not a nice thing to do. He could tie her up, he thought, as he watched her stuff her pockets with necklaces, but she might not take that too well, either.

"I aim to make some money out of this," she remarked, and that seemed to settle everything.

A stranger might have thought Lydia Parkens was the dearly beloved matriarch of the town and not the madwoman she'd been thought to be as recently as the day before. The ladies who filled her small cottage were deferentially positioned in circles about her. Slocum reflected that though he'd spent just a week in the town, he no longer was as handicapped as he'd been as a stranger ignorant of the convoluted and incestuous history of these people. And though the ladies had suddenly become solicitous of the widow, they could just as easily turn on her if they thought she was reverting back to her old obsessive feud with McBean.

"My savior, Mr. Slocum!" the widow called out upon seeing him.

He tipped his hat. "You feelin' all right, ma'am?"

"The doctor here has just checked my wound. There's a good chance I shall pull through."

The ladies about her cooed at her fortitude.

As Mamie moved to pay tribute to Lydia, Slocum walked the doctor to the door. "No need worry about injury," Doc Chin told him. "Injury like children falling on knees. Ha, ha. No fever, no pain. Just sympathy. Ha, ha. The sister,

McBean's wife, she have fever . . . Fever but no injury. Ha, ha."

"Mrs. McBean? She's ill?"

The doctor nodded his head. "Yes, fever. Crazy fever. Not ill. McBean sends men to take me from my bed. Three rough men. They take me to house far, far in woods, late, late at night. I say, 'I don't go. Come tomorrow. I sleep.' They won't go, won't take no. I go. No injury. No trouble with body. No treatment."

"They must've thought she was perty sick."

"No infection," the doctor repeated, growing annoyed. "No symptom, just fever. Crazy."

"No symptoms?"

"Chinese proverb say able woman can clean house with eyes closed, but only a crazy woman does."

"She was cleaning her house with her eyes closed?"

"Asleep, asleep, but no rest."

Mamie, meanwhile, had the ladies mesmerized as she retold the story of the Martinsons' murder in a version that diverged quite a bit from fact.

"Yesterday, Slocum forbade me to breathe a word about what really happened," she said. "That is till he was sure Mr. Denahee had gotten Evan Baines safely out of town. Now I can tell you: It wasn't the Indians that killed the Martinsons. I know for a fact this is true, 'cause I saw them bandits chasing Evan out of the dry goods store with murder written all over their faces. Slocum and I'd run around to the back of the store, you see, after we heard them screaming, 'Fire,' when we were all at Mr. Duncan's funeral mass. But the bandits had chased Evan into those crooked streets the mining men live in, and we couldn't find a trace of 'em. It was me that suggested Evan had maybe come to you, Lydia, on account of you learnin' him the Bible every Sunday. I guess them sneaky bandits overheard me and that's why they came to you—to ambush little Evan Baines."

The doctor shuffled away, and Slocum drew closer to listen to Mamie.

"I haven't gotten to the worst of it. Lydia, perhaps I shouldn't go on. At this moment, when you're recuperating from a bullet wound, I'd hate to open up another kind of wound."

"Oh, but you must go on, Mamie," the ladies implored.

"Don't worry about me," the widow demurred. "With everybody being so kind to me, I'd hate to have you disappoint them."

"I don't know if I should. I couldn't believe it, at first. I didn't want to believe it. But I've pondered long and hard over it, and I know Evan Baines told me the truth—painful though it is."

"Tell us!" cried the ladies.

Slocum interrupted. "Mamie, it's up to a court of law to prosecute this case," he reproached her. "It ain't the ladies' place to have to hear about murders and all. In any case, wait till Denahee comes back with the law before you reveal what you have to. After that, it'll be up to these fine ladies' husbands to pass on the news to their wives. A man might not want his own wife hearing 'bout these things."

Slocum felt that Mamie had said enough. He didn't want her to start making things up, and the point that the bandits had killed the Martinsons had been made. Now if McBean and Blacky insisted it was Indians, these ladies would have good reason to doubt them.

"Nonsense!" the hatchet-faced gossip declared. "Go on, Mamie. Tell us. What did little Evan Baines reveal?"

As the ladies encouraged Mamie, Slocum held his arms up, trying to regain order. "Listen, ladies," he said, though no one was paying him much mind. "It's terribly important for you all to use caution for the next few days. Keep your children off the street. There may be gunfire, and I don't want anyone to get hurt."

The ladies encircled Mamie to block out Slocum. She looked from face to face, the suspense rising. One of the women would need smelling salts regardless what Mamie said, the excitement was so intense.

"All right, I'll tell you." Mamie paused dramatically and then continued. "Evan Baines overheard the bandits say . . . They said that McBean was paying 'em to kill off those merchants he owed money to, to clear up his debts. That's why, Evan told me, those bandits had murdered his own father, Banjo Baines, on the path to McBean's, night before last."

There was a stunned silence.

"McBean," the widow murmured, aghast, looking at the other ladies to see if they believed what Mamie had said.

"You can imagine how worried that made me," Mamie continued. "All I could think about was how he'd just run up a big bill on his wedding dinner. You, Mrs. Falk, better take care. Didn't you make that splendid veil for Angelica?"

The hatchet-faced gossip said indeed she hadn't gotten reimbursed yet. The rest of the women shared with each other how much McBean owed them.

"I got my boy Fat Sang to run over to the jeweler in Chinatown to have him make me up some amulets for my cooks, I got so frightened," Mamie confided. "Not that I'm superstitious. But it can't hurt." She pulled out a couple of the twine necklaces, each drooping with a tiny gold bead. "The Chinese believe they protect against giants—and Fat Sang figured McBean qualified."

"Oh, give me one, Mamie," the widow pleaded.

"I'd like to give one to you," Mamie said. "But then I won't have enough for all my cooks."

"I'll pay for it, Mamie, and you can have that jeweler make up another one to replace it."

"Okay, okay," Mamie relented. "But I'll only charge you what he charged me—and he gave me a special price, 'cause I had him make me up quite a few of them."

"Let me buy one, too," the other ladies all clammered in unison.

"And I'll need another one for my Cole," the veilmaker's wife added, and the other ladies all placed orders for their husbands and children as well.

Slocum complimented Mamie on her merchandizing techniques as they strolled back to her place.

"Sometimes I order up jewelry to sell to Flo's girls, and this time my man got the order all wrong. Instead of a necklace with twenty-four gold beads, I got twenty-four necklaces. Been wondering what to do with them all week! Sure glad they'll make the folks rest easier tonight."

"Hmm," Slocum murmured, declining to mention that it was she who'd scared them in the first place. "What happens when word gets back to McBean about that story you told about him? Don't think you'll be sleeping too well yourself."

"Why? Next to you I'm sleeping better than I have in years. Besides, the truth needed to be presented in a clear way, like I told it. Otherwise, people get confused and come up with their own crazy conclusions."

Slocum couldn't argue with such logic. Instead he tried to imagine how he was going to go about protecting her. "It might be time to close down your kitchen and resettle some of your borders someplace else, unless you've got another good story to tell the miners." Slocum was thinking in particular that any miner who'd heard Banjo brag of how much he'd gotten paid wasn't liable to buy Mamie's story to the merchants' wives.

Mamie considered the idea for a moment. "These miners are loyal to McBean. I don't think there's a thing I could say that would change their minds. He's been a kind of underdog, and the men relate to him and like to see him getting more powerful—no matter how he goes about it."

"Then how about keeping them out of your house for a while? They won't like to hear you've been slandering their hero."

Mamie dismissed the problem with a wave of her hand. "I don't tolerate misbehavior under my roof," she said. "And besides, the miners aren't about to harm their Mamie, the woman who feeds 'em."

Slocum found her overconfident about her culinary abilities, and he mused that, like most working people, she was perhaps making a mistake by considering herself irreplaceable. Again, there was no easy way to rebut her. Instead, he just rephrased his fears.

"When McBean returns," he said, "I imagine he'll want to get me out of the way before the law comes. He knows I have friends in Lewiston and will be a formidable opponent once the cavalry is here to back me up. My guess is that he'll recruit Pick or Treleaven, 'cause they're under the same roof as us, to launch the first attack. Seems like common sense to move 'em out now while we can get 'em to leave on their own two feet."

"They wouldn't dare stir up trouble in my place," she said flatly. "Believe me. I know these people."

A gust of wind ducked under her skirts, nearly lifting her off the ground. "Looks like that storm is about to hit hard," she observed, deftly changing the subject. "I hate to sound greedy, but there ain't a thing I'd rather do than cosy back beside you in bed."

She angled her face in front of Slocum's, and he kissed her there on the street while the snow fell over them with renewed force.

He had planned to search the horse sheds in town in hopes of finding the silver stallion, but that would have to wait.

A half hour later, Slocum was deep inside Mamie when Fat Sang interrupted them. A couple of men had come calling on Slocum, he said. Though Mamie was loath to release him, she would have to wait.

7

The two men waiting to see Slocum sat on a bench in Mamie's dining room, their hats perched on their laps. They stood as Fat Sang led Slocum to them, each with his arm extended.

"It's good to have you in our town, Mr. Slocum," the first man said with measured tones. "Allow me to intrude on your precious time, if you will. My name is Francis Tucker and this is Cole Falk."

Tucker was the undertaker with the graying goatee for whom Slocum had already developed a distaste. Falk was even smaller, with a smudge for a mustache. Slocum recalled his wife, the hatchet-faced gossip. Both men sported Mamie's necklaces over their suits.

"We are troubled in our hearts about the sad misfortune that has befallen our brother Banjo Baines," the undertaker began.

Meanwhile Falk was shaking his head and echoing Tucker nervously. "We're real worried," he said. "It's a crime."

"We raise up our eyes, not our fists, to the Lord. We know there is a mysterious purpose for our trials and tribulations," the undertaker continued.

Falk began sniffing, pulled a handkerchief from his lapel, and blew his nose.

"Is there anything I can do?" Slocum asked, growing impatient.

Tucker sighed with relief. "Indeed, if you would lend your brothers a hand . . ." Falk sneezed.

"Tell me. I'd be glad to help out."

The undertaker prodded Falk with his elbow.

"It's the body, Mr. Slocum. Banjo's body."

"We don't think it right that Mr. Baines is out there under the elements like a pagan, instead of safely and lovingly resting in our hallowed ground."

"How many men you got to go looking for Banjo's body?" Slocum asked.

"Four other men right outside," Falk said, pointing with his hat. "But we could use help from a man who knows how to use a gun, in case we run into trouble."

"Reckon I could lend a hand," Slocum offered, and went back to Mamie's room for his buckskin jacket and the Stetson.

"Aw, you ain't leavin' me?" Mamie whined. "Slocum, you'll give me a pain in my love region if you don't come satisfy what you started."

"Mamie, I've been satisfying you for hours . . . and still you ain't satisfied?"

"I reckon you're right," she said, getting out of bed, stepping into her pantalets. "You'll be back for supper, won't you? Can I make you something special?"

Slocum marveled at the near perfection of the voluptuous woman before him. He'd never met a woman who was able to set aside her own wishes so readily to focus in on his. If only she were a better cook.

Outside, the shopkeepers made a sorry-looking troop, only surpassed in woe by their nags. Slocum gave them an encouraging smile and hearty handshakes in an effort to buck them up.

Cole Falk, the veilmaker and the diminutive leader of the brigade, looked eager to share authority with Slocum. "Us merchants and craftsmen of Snake Gulch got a right to live, too," he said. "If a man's got debts to pay, he ought to pay 'em, not kill the debt-holders. We need some law and order in this town." Then he blew his nose loudly. "Pardon me."

"Are you intending to take on McBean?" Slocum asked, incredulous.

"Are we?" Falk asked his colleagues.

None of them would answer definitively.

Slocum figured they'd been given their marching orders by their wives. They wanted to be protected from McBean, but left to their own devices, they'd never have come this far.

"The law's comin' soon as this storm blows over," Slocum said. "And McBean's out tracking Betcham. So let's take it step by step and concentrate on looking for Banjo's body for now. And why don't you all slip those amulets inside your shirts so you don't lose 'em."

As the men readily complied, Falk spoke up again. "Slocum," he said, "we're willing to do whatever you think best. In fact, we'd like to deputize you to keep an eye on things till the law gets here."

Slocum declined the honor. "This is your town, not mine," he said. "I'm nobody's hired gun today. But I'll keep helping you out, so long as you're willing to give justice to all people—shopkeepers, miners, the mining officers, and the Indians, too. Justice for everyone means letting the law sort out matters. Let's pledge allegiance to the flag, not to the most powerful individual at the moment."

Fat Sang came to the front of the building with Mamie's chestnut gelding, saddled for Slocum to ride.

"You still itchin' to look for Banjo's body?" Slocum asked. "Looks like the storm's getting mighty fierce."

"It's our obligation to God," the undertaker put in.

Slocum couldn't help but think Tucker was acting in self-interest, but the others agreed to brave the weather though they had nothing to gain.

"Little Evan Baines said his pappy was killed on the path to McBean's," Falk put in. "Let's find him!"

Slocum was glad the final rallying cry had some basis in reality. He had been taken aback at how these people had adopted Mamie's mixture of fact and fiction with such conviction, just as easily as they had earlier swallowed McBean's lies about the Indians. Clearly, these were people who needed to be lied to.

The snow was bearing down heavily on the procession as they wound their way up the path. Slocum expected nothing to come of their efforts. Since the murder, several people had traversed the path without discovering Banjo's body, and the drifts were much higher now. He declined to point this out, though. Even if they couldn't recover the barkeep's body, the trip would not be wasted.

As he suspected, the blanket of snow yielded no clues. The rolling terrain, fallen deadwood, and the sorry barkeep all lay under a swirling whiteness. At McBean's, the group was cold and ready to turn back, but Slocum was able to persuade them to stop inside the house. He overcame their natural reluctance by arguing it would be best to warm up before continuing the search on the return journey.

There were no guards posted outside McBean's, unlike the last time Slocum had been there, but the Indian stable hands were still hanging by their legs—what was left of them.

The sight made Slocum nauseous; he could only guess what his less hardened followers were experiencing. But glancing over their faces, he was surprised at how calmly they regarded the half-eaten corpses.

"Looks like them coyotes made a meal of them Injun boys," one remarked. The others nodded their heads thoughtfully, pointing to telltale signs, such as the missing organs and entrails.

"Since we didn't find Banjo's body, I propose we take back these two for burial," Slocum said.

"But them is heathens," complained the blacksmith.

"Matthew was a Christian, I believe," Slocum answered steadily, hoping his tone of voice would convey his seriousness of purpose.

"Still, he was born a heathen—no two ways around that," the shoemaker put in.

"And how we gonna tell one from the other, anyways?" Falk added.

"Mr. Slocum," Tucker intoned, "we don't bury murderers in Snake Gulch. Not in our consecrated ground, at least. It's God will that—"

"Listen, you all," Slocum said. "These young men did not kill Duncan, and we're going to bury them. Justice for all is my terms. You have any objections, let's hear 'em now."

"They didn't kill Mr. Duncan, then who did?" Falk asked. The other men also voiced the question.

"Same man who framed and killed them—McBean, with the help of his wife." Slocum wished his evidence were better than it was. These men could not be expected to appreciate the subtle indications of McBean's guilt. In Evan's description of the murder scene to Slocum that first morning, for example, he'd mentioned that the Bowie knife was in Elk Dog's left hand. Yet Elk Dog was right-handed. Also, Duncan's body had been eviscerated by a left-handed person, as evidenced by the curve of the blade marks. Matthew was also right-handed, but Angelica was left-handed. Another piece of evidence was the fragment of McBean's shirt Slocum had found half-charred by one of the bonfires. It was the same shirt he'd worn at his wedding celebration. Why was it burned?

Certainly such bits of proof were not the stuff to convict McBean on their own. And to convince these men with facts, Slocum would have to embroider a far more convincing set of proofs. But he wasn't about to follow in Mamie's footsteps. If a man had to resort to making up stories to get by, he might as well throw off all qualms of conscience and sell snake oil.

Fortunately, the men did not ask for proof. Slocum was their leader and they aimed to stay behind him, though at a safe distance.

Slocum delegated to Tucker and his assistant the task of cutting down the bodies and loading them onto the wagon the undertaker had been towing along. Meanwhile, Slocum led the rest of his posse up to McBean's door.

While he wanted to show McBean's men that he was fashioning a resistance, he didn't want to drive his forces so hard that they would fall apart. He advised them to stay close to the door as they entered and let him be their spokesman.

McBean's front room was filled with cheap tobacco smoke and the sour odors of unwashed feet. A dozen boots were lined up beside the stove, drying out. Their owners sat at a table, wiggling their bare, scabby toes, drinking whiskey and playing poker. Among the men, Slocum recognized Pick and Treleaven, and he tipped his hat to those fellow borders.

On the couch, Doc and the preacher sat stiffly, as though every attempt at conversation had driven them further apart. Slocum tipped his hat in their direction, too.

"We came by to see if Mrs. McBean had recovered," Slocum said.

All eyes turned to the doctor, who cried defensively, "Why you look at me? What do I know? Infection I know. Sick I know. Crazy I cannot cure. Let me go home. There is nothing I can do."

Blacky appeared at the doorway to the kitchen tapping his Smith & Wesson against the brim of his hat. "Why, if it ain't Slocum—and it looks like he's done cobbled together a committee of well-wishers from town. How nice. Thanks for stopping by. We'll tell Mrs. McBean you called."

"Actually, we came up this way looking for the body of Banjo Baines. His son said he'd been shot on the path out here the other night."

"What a tragedy," said Blacky. "Everyone always did like that barman. Sorry to hear he's gone. Why, just the other night he whacked this guy . . . Oh, but that was you, Slocum, wasn't it?"

"Since we couldn't find his body, we're takin' away the bodies of the Indian stable hands. The townsfolk don't want to go stirring up trouble with the Indians, especially not while McBean's away. I got the feeling he wanted to provoke some sort of confrontation with the Indians by hanging the dead boys. And now, well, let's just say he's not around to protect folks."

"I can handle any Injun trouble that comes our way. And anyway, McBean will be back real soon, Slocum. And when he gets back, he ain't gonna like hearing you've tried to go against his wishes again."

"I think McBean has enough things to worry about other than continuing to incite the Indians. Tell me, Blacky, what's wrong with Mrs. McBean?"

Blacky had been taken off guard. There were four armed men on both sides, though Slocum's looked like they hadn't handled their muskets since the War Between the States. Blacky seemed to realize that he hadn't been treating the miners well enough to count on their loyalty if it came down to a shoot-out. The men around the poker table had set down their cards but remained in the same positions.

Blacky stepped behind the couch and traced the doctor's outline with his revolver. "Doc here ain't doing her no good, if that's what you mean. But we're gonna keep Doc around till McBean gets back, so he can ask him his own questions. Meantime, we've got him to make the lady's medicine a tad stronger."

The miners chuckled.

"You know them Chinamen have their own opium den in their end of town?" Blacky stroked his mustache.

"Sick people need me. I must go home," the doctor said, his bristling frustration barely concealing his nervousness at being held prisoner.

"Don't worry, Doc," Blacky said. "We expect McBean back anytime now, as I said before." He strolled over to the shop-keepers huddled by the door. "These are some pretty fierce-looking dudes you got backin' you up, Slocum," Blacky went on, pretending to ignore Slocum's ready-for-action stance.

He stepped up on the shoemaker's boot to peer close in his face. "Why, this gunslinger's got a twin brother mending slippers fer a livin' here in the Gulch," he said with a laugh. "Ain't you?" Blacky turned his attention next to Falk, plucking out one of the hairs from his meek mustache with one swift tug.

"Aw!" Falk reeled and sneezed.

Slocum refrained from intervening, letting Blacky taunt the men. As long as Blacky kept his bullying on this level, no one was really getting hurt. And besides, Slocum hoped it might help build a bit of backbone in his men. He wanted them to get angry. Before, they had simply been afraid and were just as likely to hide as to fight. Now they could tap this new font of strength, this anger. Unless they were too old to change.

"Cain't do much with that one." Blacky tugged out one of Falk's nose hairs next and smiled his toothless grin. "Oo, look at this one. Covered with boogers, but long and wiry it sure is. Bet ya could sew up some pretty bows with that, tailor-man."

"Leave Mr. Falk alone, Blacky." Florence intervened from the hallway doorway. "Who but him is gonna repair my dresses that you rip up?"

"Whore, shut your trap and sit down," Blacky snarled, narrowing his eyes at Slocum, as though he were still angry at some comparison Flo had made between the two of them.

Florence pouted but squeezed between the glum-looking Doc and the preacher on the couch.

"McBean's gonna be back real soon," Blacky said lamely, for the third time. "He ain't gonna like to hear about you bustin' into his home like this, talkin' 'bout takin' away them murdering Injuns. No, he ain't gonna like it one bit." Blacky came up close to Slocum, stroking his Smith & Wesson.

"Yes, so you say," said Slocum. "Well, give our regards to Mrs. McBean. We'll be pushing off. Come on, Doc. We're taking you back to town."

Blacky cocked the trigger of his revolver, but Slocum's right fist had already made contact with Blacky's jaw, sending one of his few remaining teeth flying across the room. A solid left upper jab knocked his head the other way, and he crumpled to the ground and into unconsciousness, his revolver firing toe-level upon the men at the poker table.

Treleaven yelped.

"Gimme some rope," Slocum ordered his wide-eyed shop-keepers. One went out to his horse to fetch it. Treleaven nursed his bleeding foot, wailing like a baby.

No one else in the room moved as Slocum and the poker players exchanged belligerent looks.

"I hate to do this to you boys, but I'm gonna have to ask you to set your guns down on the floor real gentle. I don't want anybody comin' after us on the trail. Wouldn't want anybody else to get hurt."

The men hesitated. Slocum hooked his thumb into his gunbelt. He didn't really think they'd be coming after him, but he didn't want to make it easy for anyone to prove him wrong.

"Don't worry about your firearms, boys. We'll look after 'em till the law comes from Lewiston. You heard about that yet? Sure, the government's concerned about protecting your jobs at the mine. Mr. Denahee will be coming back soon, real soon, maybe sooner than McBean, and he's coming with the cavalry to make sure there are no more incidents with the Indians—or whoever's causin' this trouble. You all still work for Denahee, don't you?"

The miners began grudgingly tossing their guns onto the floor.

"That's the spirit," Slocum said. "We don't want any more accidents happening, do we, Treleaven?"

Treleaven, nursing his foot with his one good hand, bobbed his head up and down, but left his gun in his holster.

"Mr. Falk, I know you're achin' to collect those guns," Slocum said to the sniffling tailor. "Go help Treleaven get rid of his while you're pickin' up the others. Don't be shy. No one's gonna get in your way."

Slocum turned to the doctor, who had watched the proceedings with a tight-lipped air of vindication. "Doc, why don't you go over and take a look at Treleaven's foot? Ain't you the lucky one, Treleaven, to have Doc on hand?"

Tucker came in with his assistant and the shoemaker, who brought the rope. "The job's done," Tucker reported to Slocum.

"We've loaded up the wagon with the remains of them Injuns, um . . . them dearly departed Injuns."

The shoemaker handed Slocum the coil of rope.

Slocum held it back out to the shopkeepers. "Anyone care to give Blacky a proper tying up?"

Falk, all puffed up after sweeping the miners' guns into a sack, eagerly volunteered.

"Might be fittin' to hog-tie him," Slocum said playfully, " 'cause we're gonna have to find a pen to keep him in for a day or two. But since I have to ride back to town with him on my horse, you better just get him bound up, Falk, so I can swing him over the saddle."

Blacky began moaning as Falk set to work.

"Muzzle him, Falk, I've heard enough out of him today."

The shopkeepers were glowing, but the miners were glowering.

"Don't be mad at me, boys," Slocum said, waving his finger. "Blacky set his mind on having me shoot him dead, but I'm choosy about who I kill. Anyway, I like to leave shooting a man for the last resort, and he keeps givin' me too many other options."

"You yellow or something?" the big, bald miner called Tubbs asked.

Slocum winced. "Truth is," he said, placing his hat over his breast, "I'd feel bad killing even mole excrement like Blacky here. Imagine his mama hearin' the news and her thinkin' on him like he was when he was an innocent little babe in swaddling clothes. Perty sad stuff. And if Blacky here could change from that sweet lovable infant into this monster you now see, who knows that he might not change for the better over time? Do you agree, Preacher?"

Laboite rubbed his flapping jowls. "Someone pour me a drink and I'll think on it," he muttered, still planted on the edge of the couch.

Flo elbowed him. "Just agree with the man, you drunk," she said. "Let him keep Blacky out of trouble for a couple days and give us all a rest."

"I'd still like a drink to think on it."

Slocum tipped his hat to Florence, and then to the miners. "Reckon we'll leave you to your thinkin' then. You coming, Doc?"

The doctor finished bandaging Treleaven's foot. "Two toes more or less, no matter," he comforted Treleaven.

"Better leave some of your opium for Mrs. McBean," Pick put in. "McBean ain't gonna like you not taking good care of his woman."

"Come on, Doc. Let's you and me take a look at the lady of the house. Falk, anyone tries to take back his gun, you kill him, hear?"

Falk sat down in a chair, keeping his musket over his lap and his handkerchief over his nose.

Flo popped up from the couch. "Oh, I'll go with you. I've been sitting at her bedside through the worst of her illness."

"No ill," Doc muttered.

The hallway to Angelica's room was far cleaner than Slocum remembered it. Even the corners of the ceiling had been swept free of cobwebs. Slocum remembered that the doctor had said she had been cleaning in her sleep, but entering her room he was completely taken aback.

Angelica was on her knees scouring the floor with the hem of the formerly thrilling scarlet dress she was still wearing. Her hands were bleeding, so violently was she rubbing, and her hair was a mad tangle. Saliva was caked at the edges of her mouth. She was mumbling, "Fingers cry to me in bloody teardrops and mix with his in viscous paint upon the floor and in my veins and in my loins. The wretched monthly smell I cannot hide. Flow, flow, flow, flow . . . there is no perfume to mask this awful stench of blood abounding!"

Florence rushed up to her. "Aw, Angelica. I don't got no perfume on me. Aw, and you're ruining your clothes. Come back to bed."

She appeared not to have heard, and when Florence touched her shoulder, she merely returned to her scouring.

The doctor looked at Slocum. "Every time she sleep, she clean. Crazy. Nothing I can do."

"Fine," Slocum said. "Then we'll just be going. Take care of her, Flo."

"But what do I do?"

"Tie her down till fever go away," Doc advised.

"Ain't you gonna leave us a little opium, just in case?"

"No, no, no. And no more laudanum. No good for crazy!" The doctor threw up his hands, walking out the door.

As Slocum went to follow him, he heard Angelica whisper "Delivery boy" in a pathetically hollow voice. "Come, come, come, come. Gimme a pat, a pat on my bum." It looked like the rigors of marriage had taken its toll on the fading beauty. Slocum felt sorry for her in spite of himself.

Once back in town Slocum's posse broke up. Slocum left Blacky tied up and locked in a second-floor room of Duncan's house. The shopkeepers agreed to take turns guarding the door while Slocum and the undertaker and his assistant continued on to the falls to bury the Indians.

Slocum had wanted Laboite to say a few religious words over the bodies, and had taken him back to town for that purpose. By the time the men had gotten to town, however, Slocum was sick of Laboite's mewling for alcohol, and refused to employ his services.

It was late afternoon when Slocum reached the falls. The weather had changed and the snow had warmed into a steady drizzle, making the prospect of digging a grave in the rocky soil even less attractive. Slocum persevered, taking turns on the shovel with Tucker's lanky assistant. With each stubborn load of dirt, he had to remind himself that keeping the basic standards of human decency was indeed important. No matter how tiring, his work on God's acre was essential.

Tucker dawdled outrageously in his task of preparing and carrying the tiny bodies of the women down to the foot of the falls, thereby avoiding the backbreaking labor of helping dig the grave. His assistant was hearty and in jolly spirits. "We could use a spade to get these rocks loose, but we'll just have to call the shovel a spade and do our best," he joked.

He was almost as muscular as Slocum, though, and by their taking turns, the hole was dug as quickly as was possible with one shovel.

Because the ground had been so unyielding, Slocum had decided to bury all five corpses together. Back at town he had asked Mamie how to deal with the bodies. She proposed an elaborate ceremony, but conceded that under the circumstances, the best Slocum could do was to wrap the bodies in blankets, which she provided, and to cover them under a simple mound.

"Do you wish me to put forth a sentiment or two on this sad occasion?" Tucker asked, after arranging the bodies in the hole.

"Let's just fill the hole back in," Slocum said. "It's getting late."

As the assistant began shoveling back the dirt, Slocum reflected upon the short lives of Matthew and Elk Dog, the long lives of the sisters, and the violent ends they all met at the hands of McBean. Just as he was wishing for a tender reminder of human caring to relieve him of his hard thoughts, he spotted Mamie coming through the trees.

On her arm she supported the widow, and following them were the storekeepers and their wives and children. The procession moved with the appropriate funereal slowness, gathering around the grave with bent heads under black umbrellas. Slocum's heart sank, seeing the lanterns they had brought with them for the return trip. He had hoped to get back before dark. Mamie relieved Tucker's assistant of his shovel to toss a symbolic scoop of earth over the bodies, and then she passed the shovel to the widow.

Slocum surveyed the crowd. All of the men of his posse were present. He drew Mamie aside. "Who's lookin' after Blacky?" he asked.

"The preacher said he'd mind him, though I would've preferred him to come say a prayer, like he's supposed to."

Mamie narrowed her eyes at Slocum. "He said you told him not to come."

Slocum calculated how long it would take Blacky to scare Laboite into freeing him. Not long, he suspected.

He kept a lookout for movement in the trees and hurried up the proceedings, finishing shoveling the dirt onto the mound when the shovel was passed his way.

The Widow Parkens and a few of the other town ladies insisted on sharing their fond memories of the stable hands and the old sisters, and even offered kind words about the Indian race in general.

At the first opportunity he had to get a word in, Slocum abruptly concluded the funeral service and regrouped his men to protect the entourage on their journey back to town.

They were almost to the widow's cottage when the first shot rang through the trees.

Slocum didn't have to warn the townsfolk to get down, for, looking back, he saw all of them—women and even their defending men—pressed against the muddy ground as though they'd melted under their umbrellas. The ones with horses had ridden back far out of harm's way. A moment later their lanterns were extinguished.

The blue flame of the second shot helped Slocum locate Blacky's position, ahead where the boulders of the stream overlooked the path. From high on those impregnable rocks, any man, even Blacky, would be able to shoot a person passing below easily. In any case, Blacky would be able to hit a big target like Mamie's gelding. It was lucky for them that Blacky had shot too early. Still, if it weren't for his lousy aim, he could have picked off a few of them. Even by random shooting, though, he'd hit someone sooner or later.

"Crawl back down the path," Slocum ordered the whimpering townspeople as the next shot whistled over their heads. With some painful exclamations and cursing and much bumping into one another, they complied.

Slocum figured that the only way to get Blacky would be to come around from behind. To do that he would have to crawl through the brambles off the path, with someone making enough of a racket to distract Blacky.

"Falk," Slocum called out. "I need you."

The tailor slithered through the mud up to Slocum's side.

"I'm going round to get him from behind," Slocum whispered. "I want you to keep firing that musket, but aim toward the stream, not the way I'm going." Slocum made sure the tailor understood.

"But what if he shoots me first?" Falk sniffed and blew his nose.

"He won't," Slocum promised. It wasn't the safest bet he'd ever made, but the odds were in his favor.

"Slocum, if he does, promise me something. Promise me you'll take care of my little woman and our two little babies."

Slocum recalled the hatchet-faced virago, and almost relieved Falk of his post, which he supposed was Falk's intent. But reviewing how poorly Blacky was shooting, he promised and scrambled to the bushes, hurried on by the specter of life with Mrs. Falk and her young'uns.

It seemed like hours, but he'd heard only a half dozen or so exchanges of fire between Blacky and Falk before he was on the high ground of the path. In the gloom he could see Blacky pressed against a boulder, shooting down over the other side.

Slocum silently crept up to him and poked his Henry rifle between the miner's shoulder blades. "Drop it, Blacky," he said.

Blacky froze.

"Drop it," Slocum repeated. He replaced the rifle with his Colt revolver, pressing the barrel into Blacky's neck, hoping the feel of the cold gunmetal would add substance to his words.

"Okay, okay," Blacky relented, with a gruff laugh. "There, I dropped it. Now, get that off my neck. I'm looking forward to getting tied up again."

"I didn't hear your revolver drop, Blacky. A poor player like you wouldn't be trying to pull one over on me, now?"

"Musta fallen on a pile of leaves, but see, I ain't got it."
Blacky lifted his right arm and fluttered his fingers.

"Keep your hands up and turn around, real slow."

Blacky did, grinning toothlessly.

"Now, step aside from the rock," Slocum ordered, keeping
the Colt level with the miner's chest.

Blacky pretended to slip as he stepped to the side. His arm
lunged back to a crevasse in the rock where he'd stowed his
Smith.

Slocum fired when he saw the gun. He guessed that Blacky
must have thought him to be as bad a shot as he was himself.
Against any competent marksman he would never have had
a chance. At a far later date Slocum might feel sorry for
Blacky's mother, he supposed. Right then, though, he couldn't
help thinking that even she might not have been too fond of
her son.

The shopkeepers filed by the body gloating as Tucker loaded
it onto his wagon. They hailed the bravery of Slocum and,
especially, Falk, whom they had seen square off with death,
with only an ancient musket for defense. Despite their wet,
muddy clothes and the toll taken by the past hour of turmoil,
they were buoyant and in the mood for celebration.

Mamie turned the talk to food. "A scare like that puts the
hunger in me," she said.

Others agreed, and the menfolk turned to their wives to ask
what would be on the table for supper. The women, reluctant
to set aside their excitement to concentrate on their ordinary
responsibilities, were well primed for alternative suggestions.

"It's times like these that I'm glad I got me my boys to do
my work for me," Mamie declared. "If anyone's interested, I
think I can convince them to make up one of their three-dollar-
a-plate specials. Just a dollar for the children. And considering
what we've gone through, I don't think I'd care to insist that
anyone has to get cleaned up for it, either."

There was unanimous support for the idea. Not only were
the women happy to have someone else do the cooking, but
men and women alike wished to prolong the fellowship they

had forged and to celebrate their strength at vanquishing their enemies.

The air smelled sweet as the throng approached Mamie's. As the shopkeepers took their seats on the dining-room benches, Mamie's staff miraculously appeared with bowls for all and kettles of aromatic soup, just as though guests had been expected. Plates of smoked salmon, swimming in oil, quickly followed.

At first there was much gaiety about the tables as the towns-folk poked fun at one another for how uncommonly filthy they looked. Then Mrs. Falk, who had seated herself next to her husband at Slocum's table, stood to address the room.

"It's about time we formed a vigilance committee to look after our well-being," she said. "Mr. Duncan promised to look after us—and he couldn't even look after himself. The United States government doesn't know how to deal with us, being too busy redrawing their maps and appropriating and running off with funds to manage our territory. We've got to do it for ourselves."

"Let's make Slocum our marshal," someone cried out, and the move was seconded by other tables.

"Slocum's just passing through," Mamie put in wistfully as she dished out baked beans from a pot.

"Falk, Falk, Falk!" The cry went out from one corner of the room to the other.

Falk stood to applause, but quieted his supporters by declining. "I've got a living to make," he said. "Just like all of you, I've got my family to support."

"We've got to protect our families, too," someone cried out.

A cacophony of voices, high and low, shrill and rumbling, filled the room. Certain views were aired and then picked up by others, till a consensus appeared that Falk should be elected marshal and his salary paid for by profits from the mine. The only opponents of this plan were Falk and his wife.

"I live by the needle, not the sword," Falk demurred again.

His wife took the floor. "Why would McBean pay to protect us against himself?" she asked. "We need a group of men willing to set aside their work to stand up to McBean when the time comes. As I said before, we need a vigilance committee. All you men got to band together to make sure we get paid what we're owed, and to keep them miners in line when they go shooting up the town on their drunken sprees. We womenfolk shouldn't have to worry about our young'uns getting hit by stray bullets comin' through our windows, or pickin' up the loathsome ways of them miners."

"Important thing is we got to stick together," Falk added. "When McBean done in the widow's husband, we didn't know what to think. When the Martinsons were cut down to clear them miners' debts, we let McBean blame it on the Injuns. We got to stick by our own in the future."

"What we need is a court of justice to review the facts," one man proposed.

The squabbling continued on through the meal and coffee and cigars, with the supper breaking up and not much decided.

Slocum didn't feel like bathing, so he declined Mamie's invitation to adjourn to her bedroom. "Reckon I better get some sleep tonight," he said.

"I'm afraid you're right about that," she replied, sadly. "McBean's on his way back."

"He is?" Slocum asked. Her tone had implied she knew something he didn't.

"I don't think there will be any more trouble tonight. He'll have to rest up, too. And he'll have to enlist a few more soldiers to replace the ones you've taken care of. Doesn't seem like he wants to take you on himself, does it?"

"Maybe I should go after him first," Slocum said. "Perhaps under all his blustering ways he's a coward at heart. With the support of the shopkeepers, I think I could hold him till the law comes."

"Don't count on those men, Slocum. There's ten times as many miners as them—and they all know their livelihood could easily be put to flame."

"They weren't talking that way tonight."

"Tomorrow you'll see the petty pace they creep."

Slocum noticed for the first time that Mamie had somehow managed to come through the day as squeaky clean as she always looked. "Hmm," he murmured. "You smell awful nice. Maybe I'll just try to enjoy my time here and let McBean come after me when he will."

Mamie nestled close to Slocum, but a moment later she stepped back. "Slocum, I don't know how you do it," she said with wonder. "Have you been rolling in dead animals or something?"

"Well, I reckon I buried a few bodies today. Some of 'em weren't the best preserved specimens I've ever seen. Yep, then I did have to do some crawling through the muck. Can't say what was in that muck . . ."

"When was the last time someone gave your neck a massage?" Mamie asked, leading Slocum into the kitchen, where her cooks were busy cleaning up. She didn't continue on into her bedroom, however.

"I ain't takin' a bath, so don't ask me to," he objected. "The bad smell's just on my duds . . ."

"Don't be silly," Mamie said, pulling out the tin tub. "Fat Sang, boil up some bathwater for Mr. Slocum."

Slocum relented. When he really thought about the source of the odors clinging to him, it didn't seem like such a bad idea. And once settled in the tub, with Mamie's firm hands working on his shoulders, he was glad of her resolve.

"Tell me, Mamie," he said. "You sounded so sure that McBean's on his way back. Do you have someone feeding you information?"

Mamie laughed. "I listen to the coyotes, of course. Don't you?"

"You a coyote interpreter?"

"Slocum, don't think on the coyotes. If I hear anything important, I'll let you know."

8

The battle cry reverberated over Snake Gulch, from deep in Betcham's Wood, from the ravine beyond the mine, from the foot of the falls. At the grave mound beside the still, cool water, the Indian braves danced with war paint on their furrowed brows and jutting cheekbones. A flock of geese launched into the sky, past the yellow pines. Their feathers drifted down like snow and mixed with those of the bald and golden eagles, adorning the shining black hair of the men below, dancing, shrieking . . .

Slocum awoke with a shortness of breath. It was just a dream, but he did hear something sounding like an Indian attack: the faraway yelps of the coyote. He looked about. Mamie had left the room. Something had gone awry.

His clothes were missing from the chair he'd flung them over. The Colt was in its place, though, under his pillow. He checked the chamber and buckled on his holster.

Inching open the kitchen door he saw Mamie lit by lamplight, listening to the coyotes while scrubbing his clothes on a washboard over the tin basin he'd bathed in.

All was in order, after all. Seeing that he looked a bit foolish, wearing only his holster, he closed the door stealthily to return to bed.

"You awake, Slocum?" Mamie called after him.

"Uh-huh." He returned to the kitchen door.

"I need your help. Right under that counter over there is the biggest, meanest rat I've ever seen. And I've seen the best the species has to offer."

"Miss Jocund, you have turned to the right man. No rat has ever outrun my gun, ma'am."

"You can't shoot the rat, Slocum. It's the middle of the night, and the people are nervous enough. I could have shot it, in that case."

Slocum surveyed the room for likely rat-killing armaments. The butter churner and the mallet looked like a winning combination. "I woke up with a strange sensation, like something had gone wrong. Glad to see it's just a rodent."

"Ah," Mamie said. "You heard the coyotes."

"Yep." Slocum approached the counter Mamie had pointed out. He could hear the rat breathing.

"McBean's back. With Schmidt and Betcham."

"The holiday's over." Slocum poked the churning rod under the cabinet. "That what the coyotes were yelping about?" The rat raced out between his legs, slipping past Slocum's swinging mallet despite being as large as a raccoon.

Mamie reached over to the counter for Fat Sang's cleaver and smashed the blunt end down upon the rat as it ran to her feet. Her face flushed with fear. The rat squealed and Mamie struck it again and again. Not till its pointy snout was wafer-thin did she stop her pounding.

Slocum complimented her when she was finished. "That was very good."

"Not very good at all. You let the rat get by you. A bad sign."

"Oh, sorry. Reckon the gods are against me."

"Guess so," she said, disappointed.

Slocum was a bit put out, too. She was turning weird on him. Suddenly she didn't look quite so alluring with her wild frizzy hair pouring over her shoulders. She just looked like a maniac. He offered simply to get rid of the rat, and began cleaning up the mess.

"Don't mind me," she said, calming down. "Perhaps it's not that bad a sign. The rat is dead. Anyway, it's not your fault. It's just the way it is."

"Ah." The more Slocum got to know Mamie, the more he realized how little he knew or understood her.

"You better go back to sleep. I'll be back to bed soon. Don't wait up."

Slocum returned to Mamie's soft, clean sheets, and though he did try make sense of the rat and the coyotes and Mamie, he closed his eyes and his troubles vanished.

When he reopened his eyes, the sun was pouring through the windows. Mamie was drawing aside the curtains, lifting the window. "It's spring, Slocum," she said. "Feel how warm the air is."

"Come over here," he said, holding out his arms.

"No, you don't have time. You've slept half the morning away as it is."

Slocum sat up, stretched, and peered out the window at the sheds out back and the melting snow.

Mamie handed him a neat pile of clothes so bright he hardly recognized them as his own. "I wanted to keep you in the house till now. Even if you'd gotten up earlier, I'd have kept your clothes from you."

Slocum frowned as he dressed. "What's going on?"

"McBean's just hung Betcham in the town square."

"Oh." Slocum took a moment to digest the news. "Let me see. You didn't want me to stop McBean and hold Betcham for the proper authorities, is that it? You have a personal vendetta against Betcham? Wanted to see him dead quick?"

Mamie sank into the chair across from the bed. "Don't be mad at me, Slocum," she said. "I know these people better than you. I knew it was better if you didn't interfere. McBean wanted to hang Betcham for the merchants' sake. They all hated him for running away with the savings they put in the bank. If you'd tried to stop McBean, you'd have undone all the trust you built up with them."

"You may know these people better than I do, but I reckon I could have convinced them to postpone the hanging till the law came. It's just a matter of days, if that. McBean had no authority to hang Betcham."

"Whatever you say," Mamie replied tartly. "But it don't make much sense now to go crying over spilt milk. You just go out there and hold your own."

"Reckon you want me to stand by and wait for Clarkson to come do all the work, is that it?"

Mamie helped him on with his jacket. "I brushed it off, so you'll strike a fine figure. And Fat Sang's brought my gelding out front for you. Everybody's in the square waiting to hear from McBean. Sitting on my horse, you'll be looked up to."

Slocum made a wry smile at Mamie's naive optimism. "You think of everything."

"Frankly, I'm worried you might not be able to carry the high ground, even after all you've done for us. Them whores have been spreading the word that Blacky was gunning for you 'cause you treated his Flo badly. It's making the shopkeepers think you might not be so great. They blame you for putting them in danger last night."

Slocum wasn't sure how to take this news. If the people believed his beef with Blacky was really over Florence's attentions, then McBean had managed to isolate him and he was back to square one. Slocum asked about Pick and Treleaven, whether they'd come back to the boardinghouse the night before. They hadn't.

Before he left, he offered to camp out in the woods, so when trouble came, it wouldn't interfere with Mamie's business. She wouldn't hear of it. Slocum trotted into the square feeling uneasy. If Clarkson were to arrive right then, the entire town might rally around McBean, making it difficult, if not impossible, to bring the mountain man to justice.

Schmidt was finishing telling the crowd how they'd tracked Betcham through the canyons and caught him at the Seven Devils Range. He and McBean were also seated on horses, dirty and tired-looking, beside the bank. Next to them, dangling from a leafless oak, was the pale, pulseless body of William Betcham.

McBean called for Slocum to join him and Schmidt by the bank. As Slocum moved through the parting crowd, McBean also called Falk to step out.

"Let's hear it for Slocum and Falk," he said. There were jeers. McBean put his arms out to quiet them. "Come on, men," he said. "They did just as good work for you as Schmidt and me, and at greater risk. Betcham here might have been a thieving lout who tried to rob you of your gold, but he wasn't a crazy son of a bitch like Blacky.

"We miners always knew Blacky had more than his share of the devil and was aching for a bad end. He was a bad man, a rough savage. Yes, he was a real throwback. Reckon many of us liked having him around, 'cause he made us look good, and he was a reminder of the tough, raw ways of a wilder time. Those times are gone. We have womenfolk and children needing safer streets. We thank you, Slocum and Mr. Falk, for sending Blacky to his maker. Let's lower our heads for a moment to think on the passing times, and the better times ahead."

From the middle of the crowd, Florence yelled out, "Hang Slocum! Hang that murderer!"

"Now, Flo," McBean protested, "you know Slocum didn't murder Blacky. He was sniping at our merchants who'd gone off to bury them Injuns. He deserved what he got. Enough on that! If these good people can forgive them Injuns for killing Mr. Duncan, you can forgive Slocum.

"As for them Injuns," McBean continued, again raising his arms to quiet the growing grumblings of discontent from the crowd, "we are prepared should they dare to try and attack us. I don't think they will dare attack a town of hundreds of well-armed mining men. They've got their own treaty problems, besides. You've heard of them problems, how them lawyer boys from Lewiston and Boise City are making off with the government money meant for them Injuns. That's their business, and we don't poke our nose into that.

"What makes me mad is that Denahee has gone to Lewiston to get the marshal to send the cavalry to us. The cavalry! You and I know what that means. The cavalry comes out to protect them Injuns not the working man. The Gulch may be on Injun land by their reckoning, but they weren't using the gold in our Gold Hill. Them Injuns weren't about to pit their muscle against the rock and take the gold and ores God left for man to grow rich and prosper on. And there's plenty of riches in our mine."

The crowd cheered and shot their guns off in the air.

"There's so much gold in that hill that I wonder why you men are living in those shabby shanties. Are you hoarding your fortunes for the future or are you spending your working wages in the saloons and gambling houses and houses of pleasure? It's all fine with me, whatever you do with your gold. But I want you to have more, more so you can build up this town, build fine houses like Duncan's and Fletcher's over there.

"By rights this mine belongs to the men who work it. It's you who should elect the mining officers and you who should oversee the bank. More profits should go to the workers. Schmidt and I now make up the majority of the officers, and we say it should be up to you to decide who you want for your representatives. We are three hundred strong men, and if we take our rights, no one, not Denahee, nor any know-nothing marshal from Lewiston, can tell us what to do. You have the power!"

The men in the crowd waved their fists in the air, yelling their support.

"Mr. Duncan always frowned upon our daughters of joy and our merry, tippling ways. He was a civilized Eastern dude, and I ain't gonna say anything bad about Eastern ways. I'm not good enough to judge another man. But what I don't like is other people coming and judging our ways. In California, they're closing up the brothels and putting up restrictions on their wild ways. The West is getting a bit too tame for my britches when they start closing brothels. If those men from Lewiston come and close down Florence's, you people will never get yourself a wife as beauteous as my Angelica, I'll tell you that."

Slocum saw the aforementioned lady in the crowd next to Florence as the men turned to admire her. She vaguely curtsied, but Slocum was surprised by the blank expression on her face, as though she hadn't quite awakened.

"One more thing before we get back to work," McBean boomed out. "Last night I heard there was a meeting of the shopkeepers at Mamie's place. The tradesmen and their wives want a sheriff in town to keep the peace, to keep the streets safe for their young'uns. They say we miners can't control ourselves—and watching you men shooting off your pistols, I'd have to agree. But do we need a sheriff? I don't think so. Just some common sense and moderation. Please be more moderate, men."

The crowd nodded and called out its approval.

"I've said enough. Let's hear from you. You want the cavalry coming to run our affairs?"

"No!" the mob cried.

"Are we gonna tell 'em to keep riding when they push on in?"

"Hell yes!"

"I don't think Slocum's too happy with this plan. You got something to say, Slocum?"

He looked over the people of the Gulch. They were waiting for him to throw up his hands in defeat. "Do you believe McBean?" he asked them.

Slocum figured it was best to start on a positive note, so while the crowd screamed back its approval of McBean, he continued. "Sure you do. He sounds like he's telling the truth. Yet sometimes the truth ain't always so easy to figure out. Some men are very convincing, but not necessarily doing what they say they are. People say they're working for the common good all the time, when in fact they're just out for themselves.

"Justice ain't always so easy to determine. That's why civilized people have courts of law. Take Betcham here. Civilized folk wouldn't just hang the man, they'd give him a trial. The Fourteenth Amendment to the United States Constitution says no state can deprive a person of life without due process of law. We may be in a territory and not a state, but I don't see why McBean has the authority to do what no state government can. He's like a king. That's not the American way."

The jeers began in earnest, cries of "Injun lover" filling the square.

"I have personally seen McBean hire assassins to ambush Banjo and Evan Baines. He done it to them, he can do it to you." The screams grew so loud he couldn't be heard. "Reckon you don't care to listen to me anymore, so I'll leave it at that."

For a moment Slocum envied McBean's ability to sway the crowd. The law was no match for the cult of personality. But Slocum was ready to handle the consequences of giving the people the unprimed truth. He stared down the men fingering their weapons, ready to make use of his Colt if need be.

McBean quieted the mob, his huge frame reaching out as though to embrace the people. He seemed genuine, good-natured, powerful. Slocum studied his smiling, bearded face to see if it betrayed any of his murderous tendencies. Except for the black circles of fatigue under his eyes, he looked every bit the part of the champion of the masses.

"Slocum may be a stranger here and he's got his facts all wrong," McBean called out, "but we got to be careful with him. He's real friendly with the marshal from Lewiston. He's got important connections, our Mr. Slocum. He's going to get the cavalry to come charge me with the killing of Banjo Baines—who had no quarrel with me. We'll see about his due process of law when that happens. For now, let's get back to work. Let's get our gold out of the rock. Let's stop wasting time and get rich!"

The meeting broke up, leaving Slocum with only a handful of men, his posse. It was a hopeful sign.

"You still with me, Falk?" Slocum asked.

Falk looked up sheepishly. "I don't trust him no matter what he says . . . till he pays me what he owes, at least."

"Hmm." Slocum tried not to look disappointed. "Well, I expect trouble soon," he said.

The men nodded thoughtfully, almost perceptibly leaning away from him.

"Reckon McBean will be sending some new assassins my way. You'd be doing me a favor if you could secure me a space where I can hold those assassins till the law comes."

"You want us to build a jail?" Falk asked.

"Just secure me a space. It can be at Martinson's or Duncan's or wherever you see fit. I don't want to have to shoot everyone who tries something on me today." He also wanted to keep witnesses who could testify to McBean's murderous intent. It would help his case with Clarkson.

He left the men to their task. Getting a jail set up was secondary to battening down the hatches at Mamie's. McBean would aim to get him there.

At first Mamie repeated her claim that no harm could come to her under her own roof. McBean hadn't seemed that threatening in the square, from the reports she'd heard. When Slocum repeated what he'd said himself in the square, however, she called Fat Sang to get the cooks to close the shutters and board up all the windows on the first floor. As fast as they could.

"Slocum," she said. "Why open the door to trouble like this? What's the problem with you?"

"Mamie," Slocum said as kindly as he could, "I've gotta make him show his hand. Right now it's just my word against his, and Clarkson ain't about to take on the whole town if we ain't even got any proof to back me up."

"There's Evan."

"Mamie, *you* made up that story about Evan overhearing the bandits. Besides, all the miners know that Banjo's debt was paid. Banjo made a big point of telling everyone just how much he got."

"Exactly," she said. "McBean knew it was a lie and figured

he could get Evan to come clean. That's why I was never in danger."

"Maybe I should hole up somewhere else," Slocum suggested.

"What? And leave me alone?" she said. "Don't even think of it." She looked fretfully about her house, as though saying good-bye to all her things.

It was quiet for the remainder of the afternoon. Mamie prepared supper, and Slocum cleaned his Henry rifle and Colt revolver and tried to figure out how McBean would attack. Mamie was frantic, placing pails of water about the rooms to prepare against attack by fire. Slocum sat at one of her tables, a kettle of coffee at one hand and his cigarillos at the other.

At dusk the miners boarding with Mamie returned from work.

Pick and Treleaven had gotten so used to life in Mamie's house that they and Slocum exchanged polite nods despite their basic enmity. The other three miners hadn't made much of an impression on Slocum. Big and strong like all the miners in town, they were younger than Pick and Treleaven, by ten and twenty years respectively. They looked to be in their teens, actually. Callow kids, uneducated by books or experience. They were staying at Mamie's and paying her high rates because they were slow about finding their own hovel. They didn't seem friendly with one another or anyone else.

Following their ordinary routine, the miners washed their faces and changed their clothes before supper. Each had one shirt reserved for Mamie's meals. On them Slocum could read the history of the past week's fixings.

The men ate without conversation. At the meal's end, when Mamie brought the coffee, Slocum asked Treleaven, "How's your foot healin'?"

Treleaven's nostrils flared. "You did this to me. You!"

Mamie came up and stroked the back of the miner's head. "You know full well Blacky did it, not Slocum."

"That bullet was for Slocum, not for me."

"That doesn't mean Slocum shot you, does it?"

Treleaven remained silent, sulking.

"Does it?" Mamie repeated, demanding a response. Treleaven wouldn't answer, sucking in his lips to emphasize his resistance. "Did you work today?" Mamie questioned, trying a different tack.

Treleaven bobbed his head up and down.

"He got a promotion," Pick put in. "Mr. Schmidt's been trainin' him as his assistant. McBean said big men like he and Treleaven have bigger minds, too."

Mamie stopped patting Treleaven and gave Slocum a crestfallen look. Treleaven also raised his eyes at him, but Slocum didn't react, continuing to puff at his cigarillo.

"I'm sure happy for you about your promotion," Mamie said, at length. "Just don't let that Schmidt drag you into any funny business. He and that Fletcher were two of a kind, and look how Fletcher turned out."

"It's more like Betcham and Denahee were two of a kind, you ask me," Pick retorted.

"No one's asking you," Mamie snapped. "Danny, you tell me you ain't gonna blame Slocum for your foot injury."

Treleaven looked away. The three young miners stood up to leave.

"You sit back down for a minute." The men complied. Mamie continued, hands on her hips. "I'm curious to hear what you boys think about what's going on. Where were you last night?"

"I don't think nothing about it," the one with a patch of pimples on his chin declared. "We all were at Flo's place last night, then boarded up near Chinatown 'cause you'd already locked the doors."

"What about you, Pick? What's your take on what's going on?"

"Well, I saw Blacky shoot Treleaven's foot, if that's what you mean."

"That's not what I mean, but thank you, anyway. Danny, you hear that?"

"Okay, boys, enough foolin' around," Slocum interrupted. "This is serious. We're expecting trouble here tonight, so if you're going to stick around, you'd best keep to your rooms."

"It'd be nice if you'd help me and Slocum out," Mamie added. "You ain't going to be getting no sleep here tonight anyway. And either way—you help or not—I'm not going to charge you for the rooms tonight." Mamie looked about at the men hopefully, but they remained silent. "Well? What do you say? Pick?"

"What kind of trouble you expectin'?"

Slocum looked Pick in the eye, saying, "Reckon McBean's recruited a couple suckers without enough brains to know they ain't assassins. Some of 'em gonna have less brains tomorrow, believe me."

"What do we get if we stay and help protect ya?" Pick asked.

"This ain't a case of who's the highest bidder, Pick," Slocum answered. "You're either on the winning side—our side—or the losing side—and that would be McBean's."

"I'll go for the winning side, in that case," Pick said with an ambiguous sneer.

"Me, too," the young miners agreed, without expression. "The winning side."

"Danny?" Mamie asked.

"I'm with them." He pointed to Pick with his bandaged hand.

"Fine, well, that's settled then. For a moment I was afraid that you didn't appreciate me anymore." Mamie strolled into the kitchen, calling back, "How about some pie, boys?"

Slocum eyed the men after Mamie was out of earshot. "Mamie trusts you not to start any trouble under her roof," he drawled. "Be a shame to disappoint her."

The miners got up and followed one another up the stairs without responding. Under his breath Slocum sighed. "A real shame."

Mamie returned with a freshly warmed pie and asked, "Where's everybody gone to?"

"Reckon they weren't hungry."

"Them? Not hungry?" Then the truth flickered in her dark eyes. "No." She turned with disbelief toward the stairs.

"Yep. Looks like they've mistaken the losers for the winners. Perhaps you'd best be staying with the widow. Might get upsetting for you round here."

"I'm not runnin' away, Slocum. Never have, never will. Oh, those ungrateful miners. And just to think that I said I wouldn't charge 'em for their rooms tonight! It makes me sick."

"Try to calm down," Slocum advised. "No use getting all riled up about the little things when just about everything important's in jeopardy."

"It's the little things that bug me. You can do something about the big things." Mamie chewed on her cheek, trying to regain composure. "Well, what are we going to do?" she asked, gathering up her skirts.

"Just calm down. I'm fixin' to wait till they get ready to fight."

Mamie sighed.

"They won't be long."

As Slocum smoked and listened to the sounds upstairs, Mamie moved the rest of the breakables to her room muttering, "I don't believe it." She left the dining room bare, carrying away all the lamps, pictures, and knickknacks. Only the tables, benches, and one candle were left. Slocum reflected that none of his posse had bothered to stop by. They'd heeded his warning to steer clear of trouble. He hoped they'd been as thoughtful and compliant about fixing up a jail.

The sounds of the men walking about upstairs stopped. Five minutes passed.

"I think they're having trouble getting up the nerve to come down," Slocum told Mamie. "Reckon I better go on up and get this over with."

"I'm going up first," Mamie stated. "Those miners aren't killers. I know them, and they won't go against me."

"I'll go with you, then."

"It'll be better if I go myself." Mamie took off her apron and set it across the back of a chair.

"McBean controls the mine. He's a very rich man. If he can pay 'em enough to kill one man, he can pay 'em enough to kill you, too."

"McBean doesn't want to kill me, and those men upstairs won't harm a woman."

She walked over to the foot of the stairs. Slocum stood from his chair, but she pointed a finger at him to stay back. She called up the stairs. "Danny, Pick, boys, I'm comin' up to give you a piece of my mind. I don't want you bothering Slocum. I'm coming up now to whip some sense into you boys . . ."

She started up the stairs, but Slocum crossed the room and whispered, "Hold it. Someone's in the hallway." Mamie gritted her teeth and continued her ascent. Slocum came up behind her on the first landing.

They heard the floorboards creak above them.

"Danny," Mamie called out, the name catching in her throat. "Is that you in the hallway?"

There was no response except the telltale sound of Treleaven's bandaged foot dragging along the floor.

"I want to reason with you, honey. You're one of my own, you're family to me. We've been through a lot these last couple years. I don't want to see you get hurt further. Come on, honey."

"Treleaven," Slocum called out. "Do us both a favor. McBean might have offered you a lot of money to kill me, but you're not going to collect it. First off, you're not going to kill me. Secondly, if you did, McBean would never have let you keep your payment. He would let the men from Lewiston hang you for my murder. And they're going to be here soon. My friend, the marshal, along with the United States Cavalry. All I'm asking of you is to tell the marshal what bargain McBean tried to strike with you."

"I'm gonna kill you, Slocum. I'm gonna kill you!" Treleaven appeared at the head of the stairs with a musket at his shoulder.

Slocum leapt up at Treleaven's rifle, grabbing hold of the

barrel and flipping the burly miner over his shoulder and down the stairs.

At the landing, Mamie bent over him. "You never should have done that," she scolded. "And I most certainly am charging you for your room tonight, even if you spend it in jail."

Slocum glanced up and down the empty second-floor hallway. "Mamie, go get Falk. See if he's got that jail ready. I'll sit on Treleaven in the meantime."

Mamie summoned Fat Sang from the kitchen. "Get Doc Chin," she said. "But don't come back tonight. Stay in Chinatown and tell the people there to keep inside." The boy tried to volunteer to help, but Mamie wouldn't listen. After he'd left, she turned to Slocum. "What about Pick and the boys?"

"I reckon they'll have sense enough now to keep to their rooms."

Mamie gathered her skirts together and swiftly slipped from the house to get Falk. Slocum looked down the hallway grimly. "Okay, boys," he called out. "Here I come."

The hallway ran parallel with the street. Slocum's room was to the far left. Pick also had a street-side room, to the right of the stairs. The young miners' rooms, Slocum guessed, were probably facing the sheds in back.

He turned out the gas lamps bracketed along either side of the staircase. The only light was coming from the street, through the big window at Slocum's end of the hall. Pick's door was unlocked and his room was dark, the window shuttered. Slocum figured he could sit and wait for him to get back or go to his own room, where Pick was no doubt lying in wait.

Pick was the smartest of the bunch, which wasn't saying much. Not smart enough to win, but smart enough perhaps to survive and surrender. Slocum would be able to get him to talk plenty after he vanquished the young trio.

Slocum started at his end of the hall, by the window. Running down the hall, he swung open the doors to the rooms overlooking the sheds. "Game's up boys," he yelled. "Come on out!"

He'd taken the three by surprise, but they soon recovered their wits and started firing blind shots into the hall. Bullets were bouncing off the walls like a crap game in hell. Slocum took cover in Pick's room, shooting the miner in the room across from Pick's with his single return fire.

As the other two reloaded, Slocum called out, "How much is McBean paying you to get yourselves killed, boys?"

They didn't answer. Slocum didn't like their manners too much. "I said, how much is my life worth, boys? A man's got a right to know that."

"We got plenty. Plenty now and plenty more when you're dog meat."

"No, I'm real curious. How much?"

Slocum thought of the sack of gold he'd seen McBean give the bandits. He wondered what had happened to that gold. He had every intention of keeping these boys' sacks once they were dog meat.

One of the young miners came out from the room at the far right. He stood in the middle of the hall with a hat on over his red hair, a double holster about his hips, and a revolver brandished in each hand. Real tough, Slocum thought, real smart. Crouched in Pick's doorway, he had a bead on the boy so solid he could have said his rosary. "Now just set down those guns and you'll live long enough to grow some whiskers," he drawled.

The kid shot down the hallway randomly, blowing out the window at the opposite end of the hall, raining shards down upon Mamie as she came rushing back to her house.

Slocum waited till the boy had spent his cartridges. Then he made sure his Colt was visible to the boy, glinting in the light coming from the window. "Don't move, boy."

The miner froze.

"You okay, Slocum?" Mamie called from downstairs.

"I've got another prisoner for you," he called out. "Okay, carrottop. Walk down the stairs real peaceably, with your hands up on top your head." As the boy passed him, he added, "Don't try me."

It threw the miner's timing off. He hesitated while trying to reach back to slip a knife from his hatband.

Slocum shot the hat off. The boy came after him with his hands grabbing out. Slocum kicked him hard in the crotch with his pointy boot. The boy deserved a killing, but Slocum had already started feeling sorry for the other young miner's mother. It was a terrible thing to have a conscience, he reflected. He'd be so much richer otherwise.

The third one was lying low, so Slocum took a moment to drag the moaning boy to the stairs and thump, thump, thump down to the landing.

Mamie and Doc were hovering over Treleaven. Tucker looked on from the foot of the stairs.

"Are you here 'bout the jail or looking for your new customer in room seven?" Slocum asked, tying up the moaning miner.

The undertaker perked up. "Oh, have you killed somebody?"

"What about the jail?"

"It's all set up. We fortified the Martinson place. They've got a cellar that locks."

Slocum thought back to the Baines boy. That was probably where the Martinsons had kept Evan after he'd gone running to Clint for help. "Well, get Falk and some of the others to take these men over there. You'll have to wait for room seven."

Tucker hesitated. Mamie scowled at him. "You waiting for something?"

"I'll have to bring some more men over to help," he said, wiping his brow. "Maybe I should get a look at room seven first, get an idea of how big the box should be."

"Just get the men," Slocum ordered. "Afterwards you can give me back those satchels of gold you got from the bandits' and Blacky's bodies. One of them's mine and I'll be needing the other for evidence."

Tucker grew red in the face. "There were expenses, burying those two bandits."

"Sure, a couple of burlap sacks must cost a fortune. Get going. You'll get paid."

As Tucker left, Mamie looked after him, hands on hips. "I can't believe how greedy that man is. I mean, it's not as though his business is suffering any."

Slocum advanced to the pimply one's room, leaving Mamie and Doc to guard the two prisoners. There didn't seem to be anyone in the room. Inside, the curtains were blowing at an open window. Slocum stuck his Colt out the window and shot into the sky. "Stay where you are," he yelled, surveying the roofs and sheds in the backyard. "Don't move, son."

He kept looking till he spotted the miner beside the horse shed with his hands in the air. "Don't shoot, mister," the boy pleaded.

Slocum climbed out the window and hopped on the roof. "How much McBean pay you? Turn around slow."

"Five hundred in gold."

Slocum was impressed. "Yep, now unbuckle your holster. Very good. Now toss up that holster and satchel of gold. I'll look after them. Meanwhile, you go back inside and give yourself up to Mamie. Go on, she won't hurt you."

The boy threw his gun and the gold to Slocum, tears in his eyes, and went back into the house as he was told.

There was a ledge that ran around the side of the house. Slocum stepped out onto it, hugging close to the building, thinking to surprise Pick. At the hallway window the ledge was sprinkled with shards of glass. He brushed them away with his foot and heard a shot from down below. Out of the corner of his eye, he saw someone move in the hallway. Slocum ducked as a bullet whizzed by. Pick had grown tired of waiting for him in his room, Slocum realized gloomily as he retraced his steps to the back roof. He hadn't figured Pick for the stalking sort.

The pimply miner's room was still empty, so he stepped in through the window and crept to the door, to see Pick on his knees, trying to peek out the hallway window.

Pick held his pistol close to his face, as though it were a false nose. His thick blond mustache brushed against the gun's wooden handle. The barrel tapped against the window frame, shaking a dagger-shaped shard hanging over Pick's head like the sword of Damocles.

"Don't move, Pick," Slocum warned.

But Pick twitched, loosening the glass, which dove straight into his ear. It must have gone far, because blood soared out into the air. Slocum averted his eyes. He didn't much care for the sight of blood. "Doc," he called down. "You got a real challenge here, if you're up for it."

No one responded.

At the head of the stairs, Slocum saw that no one was on the landing. He descended warily.

Schmidt held a gun to Mamie's head. "The boys didn't accomplish much, did they?" he said. "McBean's decided to keep you alive, so you can smooth over matters when the law comes. Guess you could call that good luck."

On the floor lay the body of the miner with the pimples. The undertaker was going through his pockets.

Schmidt turned to carrottop, the boy who'd gotten his nuts kicked in, and Tubbs, Blacky's bald friend. "Take Mr. Slocum's guns away," he said. "And tie him up. Don't hurt him unless he asks for it."

"You can let go of Mamie," Slocum said. "I'll come peaceably."

"No. I want you to keep this image in your mind. When your marshal friend comes to talk to you, I want you to think of your sweetheart like this." He jabbed the derringer against her head. Mamie didn't flinch. "You tell that marshal everything's fine and tell him to go away. Then we'll let her go."

"Do me a favor," Slocum said, ice cold. "Tell McBean I was cut out of my mama's womb. I'm the man who's gonna kill him."

Slocum and Mamie exchanged a good-bye glance, each stubbornly refusing to give up hope.

9

Slocum knew that McBean had no intention of freeing him, even if he convinced Clarkson that he'd sent for his help for no reason. McBean had brazenly decided he could do whatever he wished. He had turned a corner and left sanity behind. The only thing he cared about was getting his murderous hands on the Baines boy. In the process, he was showing the people of the Gulch exactly how ruthless he could be.

For now it was working. People were terrified to cross him.

Slocum was disappointed to see the men of his posse moping in defeat at the doorways of their separate shops as the miners led him to Martinson's. Yet Slocum would not despair and took heart at the fresh-painted sign above the shop: "JAIL." They had tried to do the right thing.

Inside, the shelves were cleared bare. Slocum guessed that the miners hadn't had time to do the looting. No doubt the good storekeeps considered that part of fortifying the jail. Clearly the rapacity of the town's inhabitants was not aiding them in their moral stand against McBean.

Of the dozen or so miners at Martinson's, one looked more angry than the next. "Injun lover" and other crude epithets were hurled at Slocum as he was led past to the cellar. The miners' brawny arms were swelled with blood lust. They resisted their desire to tear Slocum to pieces only because they knew that McBean had other plans for him.

The cellar was pitch black, square-shaped, and sweet-smelling from the cedar walls. The fragrance stirred Slocum's appetite for a smoke. Though his cigarillos had been confiscated, Tubbs hadn't found the two Havanas he'd kept safely under his shirt. As he struck the Lucifer and puffed on the tobacco, he took a look at his surroundings.

There wasn't much to see. As upstairs, the goods had all been toted off to other people's cupboards. A thought that had been nagging at Slocum came back to mind. Ever since he'd found Evan crouched upstairs beside the broom closet, surrounded by the dead Martinsons, he'd been plagued by the mystery of how Evan had gotten there.

The boy had eluded the bandits. How? Right before Duncan's funeral Clint Martinson had told McBean that his folks had locked Evan up. Slocum had figured that much out, thinking back on the wild gestures Clint had made by the stable. His folks would have put Evan in the cedar cellar, the only room that locked. But when the killers came to get Evan, he must have already escaped upstairs.

Maybe Clint then deduced where Evan might have escaped to, but Evan stopped him from squealing with a tomahawk to the neck. Clint's mom raised her rifle, seeing her son hurt and bleeding, and the bandits took it the wrong way. Maybe.

Evan's genius was that of a prowler. He kept his eyes and ears open, and he knew how to get in and out of places. Slocum smoked and paced the cellar, surveying the ceiling and walls. He had only one more Lucifer, but the ember of the cigar helped shed a little light on the room.

The store had been built recently. Perhaps Evan had loitered about to watch the workmen dig out the cellar and build the cedar walls. If the hole had been larger than the dimensions Martinson wanted the room, a space behind the walls might have been left, which Evan might have remembered, and he might have used the tomahawk to pry the nails from the planks at that particular spot.

The cedar wood constituting the walls had been well fitted together, but Slocum eventually found the loose planks. The boy had had time to refit them to hide his tracks, but Slocum couldn't delay. He kicked in a few more planks to enlarge the hole and stamped out his cigar. As he was climbing into the moldy space behind the walls he discerned movement on the ground. A swift kick subdued the critter.

There was just enough room in the hole for Slocum's girth. A faint crack of light filtered from above, and Slocum could hear the muffled talk of the miners upstairs. The frame in back of the walls offered enough footholds for him to climb to the floorboards above him.

With his eye in a crack, Slocum had a view of a broom and a slanting ceiling. This was the little closet under the stairs going to the second floor.

Evan had relaid the floorboards over the cellar's support beams after he'd taken out the nails. It was a cinch for Slocum to slip them back out again and heave himself through the narrow opening into the broom closet.

The miners were talking about him. "We oughta jes kill him. We can take on them dudes from Lewiston."

"McBean's got the brains, not you, so clam up. You're givin' me an ache in the ear." Slocum recognized the gruff voice as belonging to Tubbs. Looked like he'd moved up in the ranks to fill Blacky's spot.

"Yeah, what if he doesn't tell the marshal what McBean wants?"

"Mebbe he don't care what happens to Mamie. I wouldn't let a woman stop me from doin' what I want."

"Can't you men shut your smelly mouths and get on with the game?" Tubbs croaked. "I mean to play out this hand before my bastard son in Boise City makes a grandad out of me."

"I'm out."

"Me, too."

"Yeah, you boys got a lot to learn about cards. Too much talkin'."

Slocum gently pushed the closet door open. The hinge creaked slightly, but the miners were anteing up. Besides the bald one, there were four miners at the table. Their guns lay beside their drinks.

"I heard they got Mamie all trussed up, tied down to her bed. That's what I heard. Some of the men were thinkin' 'bout paying her a visit later."

"She ain't no whore," Tubbs objected. "Anyone messin' with her's gonna answer to me."

"Look at Tubbs protectin' his own nigger people."

Tubbs slammed the miner's face against the table.

Slocum was tempted to take advantage of the discord to rush the miners with the broom, but he held back. It wasn't that he doubted his ability to overpower the men. He was afraid the gunplay would call attention to his escape, placing Mamie in danger.

The miner with the bloodied nose challenged Tubbs. "You gonna mess with McBean when he cuts her throat?"

"Rapin's one thing. Killin's another."

Slocum climbed back down to retrieve the rat he'd kicked. It was dead, or at least unconscious, and bleeding over the short, greasy hairs of its fur. Not nearly as big as the one Mamie'd killed, but Slocum figured it was big enough.

"Four treys, look at that," one of the miners was saying incredulously as Slocum lobbed the rat across the room.

"What was that?"

"Big rat. Just nearly flew across the floor."

Slocum heard the men shooting. He watched till all their backs were turned, and then dashed off behind the counter on the far wall.

A couple men raced in from the street. "What's goin' on?" they asked.

"Shot me a rat's all."

"Like hell! I shot it."

"Take it home and cook it for your supper, then."

"Everything quiet otherwise? Slocum givin' you any trouble?"

"Not a peep."

"Glad to hear that." A pause. "You hear the news yet?"

"What news?"

"Angelica's taken her life."

The room grew quiet. The men took off their hats. The miners who'd just come in had left the door ajar. Slocum crept toward it.

"How's McBean holdin' up?"

"He was worrying us. He ripped his shirt to shreds and held 'em out to the men, saying 'What more can you take from me?' We just felt awful. The whores had been givin' us dollar dances before the news came. Soon as they heard the news, they fell to the floor bawlin' like no tomorrow. Then McBean picks up all the chairs and tables in the saloon and tosses that furniture at them whores, telling them to get their oogly faces out of his sight. And then he turns on us men, kicks us all out, too.

"We reckoned he wants some time to hisself, so we're all headin' down to Flo's to comfort the girls. The daughters of Eve are wild in their desolation."

The men chortled briefly, but the gloom returned.

"What about McBean? Someone ought to look after him," Tubbs said. "He ain't had no sleep what with chasin' Betcham and Slocum."

"He, uh, got a bit strange. Started talkin' to Banjo Baines as though he was there workin' behind the counter. He kept sayin' to Joey, who was pourin' out the liquor for us, 'Gimme some whiskey, Baines' and 'Stop starin' at me, Banjo.' He did. Joey got the willies and lit out as fast as he could."

Slocum crawled out the door and slipped around the corner of the store and into the shadows of the alley.

He kept close to the backs of the buildings on the main street. The miners were milling about their shacks and urinating in the alley. Slocum borrowed a jacket from one of the hovels to blend in with the others, and he kept his face averted. As he approached the funeral parlor, he heard the coyotes yapping in the distance.

Looking through the window, he saw Tucker leaning back in his chair, his hands propped upon his potbelly. His assistant was grim, hard at work on the three pine boxes in the workroom.

Slocum walked in through the back door, nodding hello to the assistant.

"Slocum!" Tucker shouted, his wide eyes fixed on him with fear. "How did you escape? It's wonderful, wonderful. We were at a loss as to what to do without you . . ."

"That's why I came round to see you. Reckon we should start strengthening our resistance to McBean."

Tucker stood and began to pull on his frock coat. "I'll gather up the others," he said hastily. "Snake Gulch was in the grips of despair when Schmidt came to get you."

"I wanted to ask you about that."

Tucker fought to regain composure, but his impassive countenance was betrayed by the sweat pouring from his brow. "That time—just a few short hours ago it was—I went to fetch the men from Martinson's, from our jailhouse we'd had such high hopes for . . . a couple of miners waylaid me, put a knife to my throat, they did. Like a thunderclap of evil they overtook me, and, yea, through the valley of the shadow of death I walked. But I wouldn't say a word about anything to anyone, no matter how much I feared for my personal safety. No, not me. It was that tailor, Falk, who was the turncoat, he was."

"Then let's not round up the others. Let's just you and me stroll across the street and get rid of those men at Mamie's."

"Yes, let's. Ah, but maybe, even better, you should take the boy with you instead. He's the strong one, he is. I'm no good for fighting. And the town sorely needs an undertaker. In my line of work it's the flair for language that makes or breaks a man. If the boy gets hurt—which he won't, of course, 'cause he's fit as a fiddle—any strong-willed lad can do the physical labor, if properly instructed. Right, boy?"

The assistant was nonplussed. After meditating over his options, he replied, "As you say, sir."

"I like your helper, Tucker," Slocum remarked, approaching the undertaker with deliberate bluster. "He doesn't talk much. Reckon a flair for language might get a man in trouble."

"Trouble? No, no, no, no. It's a peaceful job, that of an undertaker. The only trouble is consoling the bereaved—and that duty is the most rewarding work one of God's children can find."

"Kind of morbid work, ain't it? A sorrowful line of work. Must get you thinkin' on your own end."

"The final reward in God's green pasture? It's not sad to think on the eternal solice of our Lord Jesus Christ."

"Reckon you lookin' forward to it so much, you've already built yourself a perty coffin for your eternal sleep." Slocum thought he might let him off lightly, just nail him into his own coffin till things settled down. But it was not an option.

"Well, ah, I may not be a young man anymore, but I'm not quite old enough to fix my mind on that."

"You're older than those three lappin' up their final rewards," Slocum said, pointing to the pine boxes.

"Gunfighters." The undertaker grimaced and shrugged.

"You have a gun?" Slocum asked. "I could use one, myself. You see, mine was taken from me."

Tucker's eyes shifted toward his desk and then to his assistant. "Get that pistol out from the chest," he ordered. "You don't have a gun, Slocum?" Slocum shook his head and ambled back from Tucker to lean against one of the coffins. He was enjoying himself, but it was time to move on.

Tucker had edged to his desk and clumsily rifled through the drawers. He turned his gun on Slocum as the assistant returned with the pistol.

"Toss me that," Slocum said to the boy.

"No," Tucker said, shaking his head. "I've had enough of your telling us what to do. I'm going to march you back to the jail where you belong, and I'll be rewarded for it plenty, and in this lifetime, too."

A shot rang through the air as the assistant sent a bullet through Tucker's mouth. He dropped to the floor, dead.

"Nice aim," Slocum remarked. "Looks like you're the new undertaker. What's your name, kid?"

"Tucker," the boy said. "Eddie Tucker."

The boy didn't look like the man's son. Maybe they were distant relations. Uncle and nephew, maybe. Slocum didn't feel like asking. "Anyone comes round asking about that pistol-fire, make up a story."

"I'm coming with you." He handed Slocum the gun he'd shot Tucker with, saying, "Take this one. It works." He stuck Tucker's silver-plated revolver in his belt.

They crossed the street cautiously, passing miners heading down the street from Banjo's to Florence's. Slocum let the Tucker boy knock for admittance to the boarding house while he held back out of view.

Carrottop cracked open the door. "What do you want?" he asked.

"Got to measure the other one."

"Treleaven? Why? Doc said he'd live the night at least. Come back tomorrow." The miner slammed the door shut.

The Tucker kid looked at Slocum.

"We'll try the direct approach," he said, stepping in front of the door, rapping on it insistently.

"I tol' you, come back tomorrow," the young miner said, swinging the door open.

Slocum's boot once again hit its mark. The boy gasped and fell to the floor.

The assistant closed the door behind them and pocketed the miner's revolver, putting his foot on the miner's neck to keep him prone.

"Watch the stairs," Slocum advised, though he didn't think Treleaven was going to be causing any more trouble. He advanced through the dining room to the kitchen door. He pressed his ear against it briefly, but heard nothing. There was no one in the kitchen, he saw, but past the open door to Mamie's room two of the miners were making advances on Mamie, which she was in no position to fend off.

Slocum hurled himself at the men pawing his tied-up

landlady. He hit them hard to the jaws, twisted one's arm behind his back till it cracked, and poked the other miner in the eyes with his fingers. Slocum's fury was such that the miners truly did not know what hit them.

They wailed and struggled to flee, but they hadn't a chance, as their persecutor hurled them one after the other headfirst against the walls.

Slocum undid the kerchief tied over Mamie's bruised mouth before cutting away the ropes that bound her to the brass bedposts.

"You sure took your time," Mamie said in reproach, pushing down her skirts and proudly shaking out her hair as she sat up.

"Sorry," Slocum apologized. "Reckon I should've been quicker at dispatching the undertaker."

"Glad to hear you got Tucker. Can't tell you how many funerals I wished it was him in the coffin." Mamie examined her former tormentors, checking to see that they were still breathing and extracting the guns from their holsters.

Slocum was unsure of how to soothe Mamie, for despite her display of bravado and feisty spirits, her mocha skin was flushed with indignation. "I'm going to the saloon," he said. "I'm gonna get McBean and put an end to this trouble."

"Your friend from Lewiston will be here early tomorrow. He's bringing the cavalry. Maybe you want to continue waiting."

Slocum ignored the sarcasm in her voice. "I was wondering what them coyotes were yelpin' about," he said.

"Here, this is yours," she said, handing Slocum his sixshooter. "Schmidt let this one have it, 'cause he boasted he'd . . ." She choked up and grabbed the other gun in both hands. "He said he'd rape me with it," she howled, squeezing the trigger. A moment later she shot the other unconscious man.

"Oh, that feels better," she said and sighed bitterly, looking over at Slocum's guarded face. "So much for due process of law."

Slocum left Mamie and the Tucker boy to do as they saw fit with their captives. If the noise from the gunfire drew out any reinforcements, Slocum would pity those hapless men.

The town had indeed been alerted to the gunplay, Slocum saw, as he strode down the center of the wide, muddy street. The shopkeepers and their families were armed and at their doors and windows, nodding as Slocum passed them.

The miners held back for the most part. One or two took potshots from the alleys and got return fire from the shopkeepers. Safely out of range, a cluster of miners poured out of the bordello down the street.

As Slocum passed Martinson's, his former guards filed out of the building. Slocum continued on toward Banjo's Saloon, and the miners kept up alongside of him from the porches, never venturing into the street.

At the intersection with the short street to the square, Schmidt and Laboite appeared, with a rigid body dragging behind Schmidt's horse.

"It's that Slocum fellow," Laboite announced drunkenly, oblivious of the friction in the street. Schmidt, however, looked about with caution, dismounted, and scurried away into Banjo's Saloon, abandoning his horse in the middle of the street.

Laboite called after him, slurring his words. Shrugging, he turned back to Slocum. "I'm feeling a little unwell," he confided with a burp. "Would you mind taking Banjo's body over to Mr. Tucker's Funeral Parlor? I'd be most obliged." He shook his jowls.

Falk and a few of the other shopkeepers came out of their stores and moved closer to see. The miners also made a tentative advance. The odor of decay filled Slocum's nostrils. He grimaced, watching the town react to the arrival of Baines's body.

Laboite kept his drooping, doleful eyes on Slocum. "I hate it when a barman dies before his time," he said. "And Banjo Baines was the best barman west of the Missouri."

One of the miners walked bravely up to Schmidt's horse and untied Baines's body. Falk followed the miner. The two men examined the body, suspending their vigilance toward each other. "He's been shot in the back," Falk announced. The crowd moved in closer.

"It's a terrible thing," Laboite lamented, "when such a generous man is killed by bandits. Why did they do it? He made the best wash and was always good for a jawbone. More'n once I've seen him give freely of his whiskey when a man couldn't pay."

"Where'd you find him?" Tubbs asked, stepping out from the porch.

"Out on the trail, coming from McBean's." Laboite noticed for the first time that the entire town was hanging on his every word. He lifted his voice as he used to in the olden days when he delivered sermons from the pulpit, liberally embellishing the stories of the Old Testament.

"Schmidt and I were making haste from that house in the woods. It is a crime against God and man to take your life. That was what I was thinking, as we rode from that house of death. What does God want me to do? Despair has overtaken our town, and women are killing themselves. I have failed to bring the nurturing words of Christ to our people. How can I bring the people together? I asked God.

"God answered my prayer. He sent me a dark angel, an owl, big and dark and ominous as death itself. In its talons it carried a strange-looking beast. What is that? I asked God. And He heard me and told His angel to drop its burden to the ground.

"I stopped my horse and so did Mr. Schmidt, both of us in awe of the omen, the warning of what we could not say. Mr. Schmidt held up the beast and just as our eyes were fathoming its terrible identity, a still more horrible sign hit us from Heaven, carried upon the currents of the air."

The townspeople, miners and storekeepers, faithful wives and prostitutes, had drawn up to Laboite, who flung his arms toward the sky.

"Lord! Why have you laid before us the vain toupee of Banjo Baines? What is this foul smell overtaking us? Is it because of our vanity that you hate us? Are we thusly punished for strutting about as though You had not seen fit to make us bald?"

The crowd shifted restlessly. Tubbs sallied forth. "Oh, go get yourself another drink," he said.

Laboite saw he was losing his congregation and flung up his hands again. "Lord!" he cried again. "Why have you stopped us, if not for to find the body of Banjo Baines? The owl hooted once, twice, thrice, as though to remind us that Banjo Baines was one of the Lord's sheep, and that He wished to see our beloved barkeep placed in consecrated ground so his soul may be freed to join His Master. The divinity of the Lord is spread to one and all through the mercy of Jesus Christ our Savior. Amen."

"Amen!" the people shouted.

"Look!" Falk cried out, holding up a small pouch. "The bandits, if it was bandits, didn't even take his gold."

Laboite hung his head toward Falk and whispered, "Do you think we could pass around a hat for a collection? Maybe you could start it off."

Falk didn't have time to consider the question, for McBean had wended his way bare-chested through the masses, holding onto a bottle of whiskey, Schmidt at his heels.

"What is this circus here?" he asked. "Have you brought my poor, short-lived bride?"

"No, my poor wifeless son," Laboite continued, in his oracular vein. "She is still upon her couch where she took her poison."

"Then, what is this all about?"

"It's Banjo Baines. Shot in the back," Falk said challengingly, his little mustache twitching from his runny nose.

"Impossible!" McBean boomed. "My pal Banjo is back in his bar, pouring out his whiskey, consoling me on my loss. There he is, see? At the doorway, pointing that finger of his at us. He plays at seeming mad at us, but no man has a readier laugh."

Some of the miners began drifting away, back to their

shacks, shaking their heads. The storekeepers, too, stepped back. A great silence descended over the street.

McBean examined the body more closely. "It is Banjo!" he declared, and pulled at his beard. "I'm going mad, mad. Tormented by ghosts, plagued with sleepless nights and disaster all around. All my plans, nothing. What is life without Angelica? Without sanity?" McBean looked at the townspeople with a terrible intensity. The dark circles under his sunken eyes made him look as deranged as he sounded.

The shopkeepers drew Laboite and Baines's body away from McBean, to the side of the street.

"That's it. Take him away. I'll no longer be haunted by his condemning ghost. What's this? Slocum, is that you, or do my eyes deceive me again?"

"Flesh and blood."

Schmidt summoned a few of the miners who hadn't abandoned McBean. "Take this man back to his cell," he ordered.

"Stay where you are," Slocum countered, over his shoulder. "Schmidt, if I were you, I'd keep out of this. I haven't forgotten your pushing me over the falls, and my patience is worn thin. Right now I'm talking to McBean."

"Yes," McBean muttered. "You stay out of this, Schmidt. Slocum wants a showdown with me." McBean stroked his beard. "I do understand you correctly, Slocum, don't I? You don't just want to talk, do you?"

"I'd rather you come with me peaceably. I don't much enjoy killing folks. Maybe the law won't hang you. Maybe they'll decide you're sick in the head and put you in a loony bin. It's up to the law to decide."

"You know you can't kill me. Not till Betcham's Wood flies before my eyes will I come to harm."

Slocum drew fast, swiveling toward the porch and pressing the trigger of the Colt. A miner who'd raised his rifle fell lifelessly into the street. Slocum called down the street, "I don't think you understand me. When I say I don't enjoy dispatching you all to hell, that don't mean I won't do it if provoked."

"You provoke them, too. You're a stranger here. You butt

your nose into our business and start killing folks. You moralize about me and us miners, telling us not to kill. By what rights do you justify your own killing?"

"You're coming with me peaceably now or they'll be getting a wagon to fetch you."

"Murderer!" a shrill voice cried from the other side of the saloon.

Both Slocum and McBean turned to see Lydia Parkens shouldering her musket despite her sling.

"You killed my husband," she screamed. "And I blame you for tempting and leading my little sister to her grave."

"Someone disarm that crazy woman," McBean sighed. A couple miners grappled with the wounded widow, wrestling her to the ground and finally wrenching the weapon from her grasp. "Don't hurt her," McBean admonished them. "Just tie her up and toss her back in her house. In the Bible a man's expected to marry his dead wife's sister. If she forces me to do that, I'll want her as intact as possible."

The miners could no longer trust McBean enough to know if he was joking or in earnest. McBean tried to laugh, but the deep rumblings in his throat were dark and ambiguous.

"You're finished, McBean," Slocum said. "Your supporters are dead or have deserted you, for the most part." He tossed a sneer in Schmidt's direction. "I have my revolver in hand and I intend to use it unless you move along down the street with me now."

"These are idle threats," McBean declared. "Go ahead. Try to kill me. You'll see it will do you no good. I will not fight a little man whose mother's hips were too skinny to bear a child as nature prescribed."

The miners were gaining heart and began to move in closer. There was method to his madness, perhaps.

Slocum considered shooting him dead, then and there. His only qualm was in shooting an unarmed lunatic in cold blood. And he couldn't very well give him a thrashing. McBean stood a head taller than him and looked formidable indeed, standing with his huge chest bared.

"My daddy was a forty-niner. Left my mama for the gold of California." McBean walked about, addressing the miners. "A fortune-teller had to tell me what became of him, 'cause me and Mama never heard from him again. But I know he struck it rich and lives in San Francisco in one of the palaces over-looking the ocean."

Slocum discharge a bullet in the air. "No more stalling, McBean. Write your memoirs in jail."

"Shoot or get off the can," McBean quipped, with a twinkle in his eye. "I feel like tellin' the men about my daddy. Come on, men, let's all get some whiskey at Banjo's." He waved the bottle in his hand to summon the miners looking on.

Slocum shot the bottle as McBean was about to take a swig from it. He looked back at Slocum with contempt. "Get someone to take care of that nuisance," he said to Schmidt, turning his back on Slocum.

Slocum aimed at McBean's boot, but all at once a core group of supporters encircled McBean and someone else took the hit. "Damn," Slocum said. It was ludicrous, but it looked like he'd have to play by McBean's rules. He didn't like it, but sticking close to McBean would at least ensure that no more trouble would occur till Clarkson arrived. And if it did, Slocum would be there to handle it.

McBean sat on the bar pouring out whiskey as the miners lifted their glasses up to him. No one paid any attention to Slocum as he swung through the batwings.

"Course I always meant to make something of myself—to follow in my daddy's footsteps, as they say. As soon as I got old enough, I took a job on the stage from Atchison to Folsom, California. Two thousand miles it was, and it took us but twelve days. First thing in California, I headed to the mines, Sutter's Mill, you name it. I'd started off looking for Daddy, but I ended up learning the promise in the grains of gold dust."

Slocum watched Tubbs confer with Schmidt at the side of the room. On the one hand, Slocum welcomed another offensive. If he could get Schmidt out of the way, he could scare off the other miners and keep guard on McBean in the saloon till Clarkson came. On the other hand, Slocum had but two bullets left in the Colt, and there was no discrete place to reload, no sitting down, as the tables and chairs had been flung to the corners of the room. Two bullets. Schmidt, Tubbs, and McBean. The math didn't add up.

"Can't say I been to every mining camp in California, but in this territory, I've seen every one of 'em. Around Owyhee and Orofino, Elk City and Pierce City. Up and down the Boise River Basin I've panned and worked the placer claims . . ."

Schmidt was approaching from one side of the room and the bald-headed miner was coming from the other. Slocum kept his back to the wall and picked up a shot glass lying nearby on the floor. If worse came to worst, he could replay his first encounter with Blacky.

"Each stampede to a new Gold Hill, I'd already be there among the first. I'd search out the old-timers in them rag towns for word of my daddy. And I'd listen to their stories of the ones who'd kept hold of their gold. You see, that's the trick of it. Many get lucky. But luck don't mean the man's prepared for his good fortune. And some men grow used to the life of hardship. They don't want no palace, no hundreds of children and wives bothering them all the time. All they want is an hour's time with a parlor-house madam named Rosita and to keep their neighbors in the groggeries and gambling houses in enough forty-rod to pass a couple days of this infernal life in peaceful recreation."

Tubbs was enlisting help from one of his pals. Slocum began to like his two-bullet-and-a-shot-glass plan less and less. He needed another gun. "I wouldn't mind a bit of peaceful recreation," he shouted, coming toward McBean with his raised shot glass.

Pushing past the miners about McBean, Slocum was able to lift a gun from one of their holsters and stick it in his waistband. Since that went so smoothly, he tried to disarm another, but that miner felt his gun being taken.

"Hey, gimme back my gun," he demanded.

Although the miners had not foreseen this turn of events, they quickly recollected their wits and tried to grab ahold of Slocum. McBean raised himself on his feet and stood on top of the bar, overlooking the action.

Slocum kicked out at the miner's shins and pushed them back, furiously knocking down the ones closest. Like dominoes, these men sent the others sprawling to the floor. Out of the corner of his eye, Slocum saw Schmidt signal Tubbs to shoot. Leaping up onto the bar as the sound of the discharge quieted the room, Slocum returned fire, shooting the bald miner in the gut.

Tubbs staggered across the room holding his belly as blood and gore came oozing out of him. Then he fell on his face, moaning and slowly dying. It wasn't pretty.

"Let's you and me fight it out with our fists, McBean," Slocum said, looking up face-to-face with McBean. "Stop hiding behind your men."

Slocum surveyed the room. The men looked to McBean for guidance. The bearded man nodded and Slocum unstrapped his holster and set it aside. McBean's first punch hit Slocum like a battering ram, sending him down the bar counter like a dish of nuts.

The miners cheered, but Slocum was quickly back on his feet, his fists up and ready for their turn.

"That's enough." Schmidt held out the derringer. "I think we know who is the better man."

The miners objected, but Schmidt discharged a shot to silence them. And then shot the one miner still objecting. Slocum dove off the bar into a roll. Schmidt was no Blacky when it came to aiming.

Suddenly Schmidt's expression changed from surprise to blankness. He fell to his knees and his head slumped over. In his back was lodged an arrow. From outside the saloon came the loud yelping of a coyote.

"The Injuns is attacking," the miners cried, scrambling behind the overturned tables and chairs.

10

Only Slocum and McBean stood, for a moment listening for further sounds, but hearing nothing.

Slocum bent to retrieve Schmidt's derringer and turned to McBean, who was still atop the bar looking invincible and smiling as though he welcomed the idea of an Indian attack.

"Gimme that rifle," McBean commanded one of the cowering miners. "Let's kill us some Injuns."

"I don't think so," Slocum called back to him. "Look at this arrow. Looks rather familiar, that wood the arrow's made of." He pulled the shaft out from Schmidt's back. "Looks like it comes from Betcham's Wood, wouldn't you say?" He tossed the arrow over to McBean.

McBean's black eyes grew darker as he examined it. Slocum read his lips mouth the words, "Till Betcham's Wood flies."

Aloud he said: "My death warrant! It's my death warrant. What them Injuns know anyway? You're not going to get me, Slocum." He leapt off behind the bar and grabbed the holster Slocum had put aside.

Slocum was moving too fast for McBean to make good on his one shot. Then Slocum charged the bar, knowing that that had been the last bullet in the chamber. McBean clicked the trigger of the Colt several times before throwing it toward

Slocum's head and running for the saloon's back door.

The miners slowly got up off the floor, astonished.

Slocum toppled McBean before he reached the door, grabbing onto his massive legs. McBean struggled free, planting one of his enormous boots in Slocum's face. Slocum got to his knees and made another lunge at the giant, gripping his legs together as tight as he could. Once again the miner managed to elude Slocum's grasp, and his shoe swung like a mallet onto Slocum's ribs.

For a moment the pain obliterated all other concerns, but Slocum came back to his senses in time to roll out of the way of another onslaught from McBean's boot.

Both men got to their feet and faced each other with fists raised. Slocum kept out past the range of the miner's long arms, hoping to catch him off balance by a series of feints to the sides.

McBean had another plan altogether. Rocking back and forth, he moved incrementally toward the back door and to the side wall, near which were stacked two towers of empty barrels. With one of his deadly kicks he toppled these upon Slocum and fled into the night.

Slocum had to let him escape, for the moment. The barrels effectively blocked the door.

"Ain't that gummy?" one of the miners said, spitting in McBean's direction. "Him jes turned poltroon on us."

"Showed us the white feather," another said, and soon the room was full of chicken-squawking sounds. The merriment was short-lived, however. Slocum could tell they'd followed the action closely, rooting for McBean till the last. They were occupying the same room, but they weren't friends.

"Don't you men get in my way," he said to them brusquely, recovering and then reholstering his Colt and heading out the batwings in pursuit.

Slocum investigated the buildings surrounding the square first. The houses were quiet, the mining office empty, the blacksmith's shop shuttered. Betcham's body hung beside the bank, telling no tales.

There were too many places for McBean to hide, and he hadn't left any clues. It was incredible that he should disappear without a trace. McBean, whose stature and girth and domineering personality were unmatched in the town. Where were the people?

Slocum rapped on the blacksmith's shop, but there was no reply. It was tempting to turn the handle and just go in, but Slocum wouldn't force the smith to talk if he didn't want to.

He went back to the main street and stopped at the tailor's shop. "Falk, open up." Silence. Then a rustling behind the door. It opened a crack. Falk's runny nose in the crack.

"Is it over yet?"

"What? McBean?"

"The Injuns is attacking."

"There are no Injuns, ah Indians, attacking."

"Young Chief Joseph hisself came riding down our street."

"You're seeing things, Falk. Come out. Look around."

"No, it's true." Falk stuck his head out the door. "He came riding down the street on the Ghost Horse, waving his fist in the air, with his face all painted red and a huge headdress that must have weighed thirty pounds. And I should know."

Mrs. Falk appeared at the door, pushing her husband out of the way. "You leave my Cole alone, Slocum. We're praying." And with that the door closed in his face.

Slocum knew one Indian arrow did not constitute a siege. He had his suspicions about what it was, but it was pointless trying to argue the shopkeepers out of their fear. It was better if they all stayed out of the way in any case. They might get hurt.

Mamie was not at her house. Slocum didn't stick around long there. Carrottop had been shot through the groin and his blood smeared about the dining room as he writhed in his death throes. It had been a bad death, but perhaps he deserved it. As for Treleaven, Slocum wasn't curious enough to go upstairs to find out what had become of him.

The Tucker boy was also missing. Maybe he was at Flo's celebrating.

Slocum walked back into the alley and through the shanty-town, but all the little shacks were dark. He was happy to find the town so serene in its dreams and prayers and whoring. Probably all the town's inhabitants were wishing McBean were dead or would go away. Perhaps he had, and no one was bothering to tell him.

The stables were a bust. McBean's black stallion was still there.

There were too many places in town for McBean to hide. Without help, Slocum didn't have much of a chance of finding him. He had one Havana and one Lucifer left. He wandered back through the shantytown, toward the mine. There, he would have a smoke and watch the sun come up. If he saw anything suspicious from the high ground looking down over the town, maybe he'd continue his pursuit of McBean. If he felt like it. Otherwise, he'd wait for Clarkson, and leave it to his judgment how much the law was willing to pay for him to bring McBean to justice. But as he kicked up the street, he felt galled that McBean had eluded him.

Crossing over the ravine to the mine, he noticed some-thing odd. The mine's portal was unlocked. In the confu-sion of the day, it was possible that someone had forgotten to replace the padlock. Yet Slocum was willing to entertain the notion that it was unlocked for a completely different reason.

He slipped inside the doors and listened, thinking all the while about Parkens, whom McBean had killed by collapsing a section of the mine on him. This was McBean's territory, and Slocum was not sure that he wanted to challenge the miner in such unfamiliar circumstances. One option was simply to wait outside the mine.

Besides the dripping of water as it seeped through the walls, the mine was silent. Slocum waited for a few minutes before lighting the Havana. It was less risky to use his last Lucifer here than out in the wind, he rationalized. He kept hoping to hear something to confirm his suspicion that McBean was indeed there.

The Lucifer illuminated a wall of lamps. Slocum resolved to light one of them, reload his Colt, and then maybe satisfy his curiosity by taking a walk around.

The mine had a wide adit, running straight out as far as the lamp's light would reach. Wheelbarrows and water pumps, picks and drills lay against one wall. Cases of Alfred Nobel's dynamite were stacked alongside a pile of timber.

A long shaft had been sunk at the opposite wall. Slocum passed the hoistway, constructed of square sets. These timbers—mortised and tenoned, fitted together as cubes and then filled with waste rock—held up the weight of the mountain, Slocum figured, continuing past them to the manway.

Here he heard a sound. Faraway and faint. But yes, the distinctly deliberate footfall of a human being. Slocum extinguished the lamp and took a couple final puffs at his cigar, peering down the manway.

The light was very far away, coming from the farthest level, sixty feet straight down into the rock. A series of rough ladders took Slocum from level to level. At each successive, deeper stage, the level would be longer, tracing the incline of the ore rock. The levels were made up of hollow square sets, with timber planks for floors and the dark rock on all sides.

The sounds of movement grew louder and louder as Slocum descended. On the sixth level, he could see just below him a lamp casting shadows on the rock floor. Slocum got to his knees and bent his head down to the final level to better see what was going on. Just then McBean lifted the lamp and turned toward Slocum, who pulled his head back. Silently Slocum rose to his feet and moved down the planking away from the manway.

As McBean climbed up the ladder, he whistled "There'll Be a Hot Time in the Old Town Tonight."

Slocum let him climb all the way up before cocking his Colt. But McBean appeared not to notice, continuing to whistle and trooping toward Slocum with a satchel over one shoulder, two rolls of wire under one arm, and the lamp in his hand.

Soon enough the lamp cast its beams over Slocum's Colt, and McBean paused.

"Ah, Slocum. You never give up." He set down the satchel and lamp.

"You can drop that holster, too."

McBean laughed. "Why should I use a gun, when I can blow you up with a touch of these two wires?" He held out two spools of wire for Slocum to see.

"Now, why would you want to blow up the mine?" Slocum asked. He tried to put out of mind the horrible thought of being buried alive. Well, at least he wouldn't be alive for long, he thought, reflecting on the satchel of dynamite.

"If there's no mine for Evan to inherit, I can undo that curse."

Slocum felt more uneasy. McBean was totally unhinged. For the first time in a while, Slocum didn't like the odds. "It's not gonna help you to blow yourself up in the bargain," he said, wondering how far gone the miner could be.

"I might risk it, though. I'm closer to the manway, and that pillar I rigged is holding up that wall directly to the side of you. No, I wouldn't want to be where you're standing."

"Doesn't matter what you do to me, McBean. The men are right outside the mine waiting to shoot you once you try to escape."

"What men? That tailor and the widow with the broken wing? I think I'll take my chances with them." McBean picked up his lamp and satchel and backed away, leaving Slocum in the dark.

"Fine," Slocum said, stepping up at pace with McBean, keeping his gun glinting straight at the burly miner. "I'll come with you."

"Remember the wires," McBean said, dropping the lamp.

Slocum dove toward the opposite wall as a shot rang out and ricocheted about the passageway. He heard McBean scurrying up the ladder and took a wild shot at him in the dark. McBean returned his fire, and then, after the bullets had come to rest, the mine was silent once more.

For a while there was a stalemate. Each knew the other would shoot him if he risked climbing up the manway ladders.

At least the immediate threat of McBean blowing up the mine was over. He had dropped the wires. Perhaps he had just been bluffing. He still had his satchel, however, so the threat was not completely over.

There were no ladders at the much narrower hoistway, but a long wire hung down the center of it. Slocum figured he could either jump down to the lower level and retrieve a stick of dynamite or shimmy up the cable. Neither plan was perfect. He didn't have a match to light the dynamite and wasn't eager to toss around explosives under the ground; alternatively, he'd be trapped if McBean heard him coming up the cable.

"Do you like our mine?"

Slocum didn't respond. The question was asked merely to get a fix on his position. It had accomplished as much for Slocum, who guessed that McBean was breathing down the manway. He aimed toward the sound and fired.

The discharge, briefly giving form to darkness, left a frozen image like a daguerreotype in Slocum's mind. The timber, rock, and McBean holding a stick of dynamite. His shot had gone wild again. The rock had shifted the sound of McBean's voice to the side.

Slocum fired again—the man was gone from the picture—and moved past the manway to the hoistway. Then a light flashed above and Slocum threw himself blindly into the hoistway, hoping to grab hold of the wire cable. He did, just as an explosion of sound and dust rocked the shaft.

Hand over hand, Slocum heaved himself up the wire cable. The first stick hadn't done too much damage, Slocum assured himself, hoisting his feet onto the fifth-level platform. Yet just as he breathed a small sigh of relief, he saw another stick of dynamite sparkling down the manway.

He held tight to the cable, hearing the dynamite rolling down the sloping passageway. Rolling, he guessed, right for the pillar McBean had wired.

The first explosion was succeeded by three more, each deafening and horrible, tearing away the insides of the mountain as though wounding a wild beast in the belly. Dust and rock bombarded the shaftways from all directions.

Slocum's arms held fast to the cable, his muscles throbbing, the skin of his fingers and palms ripping away at each successive grasp higher. And there was no breathable air, just dust, vibrating as the very walls of rock shuddered and groaned inches from his face. Slocum saw the mountain stir to bleak life, filling back up the holes that divine imagination or man in his impudence had hollowed out.

The cable seemed never-ending, yet Slocum was certainly thankful for it. His strength endured, despite the lack of oxygen and the searing pain in his palms, despite the rocks spilling down the hoistway from the loose waste rock of the square sets. The rumbling did not cease and the hoistway rattled ominously.

One level collapsed, and the rock began filling in the shaft. Each level shivered and then collapsed with a fatal spasm. The wall rock buckled just below Slocum's feet, but he increased his efforts, no longer feeling the screaming in his hands. At last he was up to the adit. The hellish groans of the earth below did not abate, however, and Slocum lost no time, but crawled from the hoistway and took to his heels.

Pure white rays, like a heavenly chord, pierced the cracks of the mine portal. The dark was vanquished. There was air. Slocum pulled open the high wood gates and a shot ripped through the wood above his head.

Slocum grabbed hold of his Colt. He wouldn't look at his hand. He knew by the way it slimed about the handle that it would not be a pretty sight. Past the edge of the door he spotted movement. It was too good to be true. He stuck his Colt out and felt a prideful certainty propelling the bullet down the barrel, straight into its quarry. He knew it would hit its mark, and rushed out from under the groaning Gold Hill.

The bullet had gone through McBean's temple. His deranged eyes were gazing downward, down at the barren earth whose dead ores he'd spent his life harvesting, and down farther at the demons beyond, whom he was joining.

Slocum left the miner where he lay and staggered back to his own room, upstairs at Mamie's. He was asleep immediately, his blackened, dust-and grime-covered body hugging the clean-smelling white sheets.

"Oh, look at those hands of his. Fat Sang, go fetch Doc Chin." Slocum felt his body being rolled onto its back. "Come on. Wake up, Slocum."

He opened an eye to the sight of Mamie fretting, hands on hips. She looked to be silently scolding him on his filthy appearance. Maybe he was just imagining that.

In fact she was cataloging his various injuries and worrying how best to deal with them. His knee looked particularly troubling, bruised and swelling out from a long rip in his trousers. "Your friend's been asking after you," she said, unlacing his boots. "That Mr. Clarkson. He and his cavalry just mosied up to town like they were out taking the air. I expect you'll want to see him soon as you're cleaned up."

What he wanted was to be left alone for around the rest of his life. He saw the inevitability of dealing with the matters at hand, however, and tried unsuccessfully to sit up at the sound of his trousers being ripped to shreds. More effort was required than he seemed able to muster.

"Just keep still a moment." Mamie chastised him. "Oh my!" she exclaimed, but didn't elaborate. Slocum didn't care to hear about it, anyway. If he appeared half as sore as he felt, he might look like one of those early Christians martyred by the lions. He struggled to sit up again and made it partway, only to be pushed brutally back by Mamie.

"You injure your ears, too?" she asked. "Or am I not speaking English? Just keep still. I'm not about to let you get out of here till I've cleaned up those wounds. If I don't, you'll end up like Treleaven, without a hand to eat with or a leg to stand on."

Slocum could see why Treleaven had turned on Mamie. He was also vaguely encouraged at the implication that Mamie hadn't murdered that miner yet. He kept that in mind while she and the doctor and still others tortured him for two hours, picking bits of rock from him and then scouring his wounds madly. Finally, Doc pasted him with herbal salves and bandaged practically half his body.

Falk appeared with his wife, and together they fashioned a loose pullover shirt and woolen trousers which Slocum's mittlike bandaged hands could pull together with a string.

"We've petitioned Mr. Clarkson to keep you on here as marshal," Falk said hopefully. "The men took a vote on it just a bit earlier. All of us—and that's including the miners, too—raised some money to get you to stay. We're going to build a regular jail, we decided, and a courthouse, too."

"That's mighty thoughtful," Slocum said, taking the pouch from Falk and dropping it into his pocket. "Reckon it'll be quiet for a while and nothing for me to do, so I'll be pushing off."

Mrs. Falk opened her mouth to object, for surely he had misunderstood. The money was for future services.

But Mamie didn't let her get a word out. "I'm glad to see you finally getting some recompense for all this work you've done for us," she said, and added, "although, it's certainly not enough. I'd guess there was maybe three hundred dollars in that pouch, if that. Why, McBean paid his killers more than that to murder you!"

Slocum buckled on his holster. "I wonder what became of that money," he mused. No one in the room had a theory to share on that subject. Slocum recalled that there had been a lot of gold in the house the night before. Not only his own pouches for returning the deed and working for Banjo, but perhaps $2,500 more, if each miner had gotten $500 for their efforts to kill him. Perhaps McBean had gotten back two grand from the miners who died before him. Perhaps all of the money was still on his body, but Slocum doubted it. Not in this town.

"Well, I best be off," he said, picking up his few belongings and turning stiffly to leave.

"Slocum," Mamie said, her voice pitched low in a tender reminder of their past intimacy. "You'll come say good-bye before you go, won't you?"

"Sure," he replied. Despite the shortness of time, they'd gotten to know each other too well. He mistrusted her. Still, they could leave on friendly terms.

Clarkson had set himself up at Duncan's house as the cavalry fed and watered their horses at the stable next door. The marshal greeted Slocum at the doorway, leading him inside the house like he owned the joint. "You always keep me waiting," he said. "But it's okay. I hear you had a hard night."

"I've had harder." Slocum shrugged. He'd never once kept Clarkson waiting. Quite the opposite.

Sitting around a table were Denahee, Evan, and a dark-haired lady wearing black velvet, with many gold buttons. Evan pushed his chair back and raced up to Slocum, crying, "Slocum, Slocum," and hugging him painfully from the side. "I knew you could kill McBean!"

He patted the boy on the shoulder. "How are you making out?" He felt bad the boy seemed to have learned the wrong lesson from him, but at least his spirit had not been crushed.

The woman summoned Evan back to his seat with a bark. Slocum had to encourage him to return to her side.

"This is Mrs. Baines," Clarkson said to introduce her, bowing with his new citified manners. Slocum remembered Clarkson from when he was a simple, charmless Texas Ranger. "You already know Mr. Denahee."

Slocum shook hands with both. Their grasps were so light he hardly felt any pain at all. He wondered if he should offer condolences on the loss of the one's husband and the other's friend. They did not appear to be in the grips of mourning, however, so Slocum remained quiet.

"Mr. Denahee and the boy have been singing your praise for days now," Clarkson said with a wry face. "In fact, I got a letter here requesting that you be made a law officer of the town. Signed by hundreds of men, if that's what these Xs signify."

"I'm itchin' to know why if you've been hearing songs about me for days, it's taken you so long to pay me a visit."

"Ho, ho. I knew you could handle this situation. And we had some nuisances of our own. Yes, we had a traveling show of lady acrobats from Mongolia raising hell in Lewiston. In any case, you've proved yourself, and now you're sitting pretty."

"Clarkson, I reckon you know I'm not fixin' to settle down. Just came to make some money and look into buying some ponies. Besides, the last time I seen the mine, looked like this was one boomtown that's gone bust."

"Oh, not at all," Denahee objected. "Mr. Duncan was going to collapse that shaft soon in any case. That vein had come to an end. But there's plenty of ore in that hill and we have new equipment coming." Denahee was waving a sheet of parchment. Looked like he'd gotten a new deed from Clarkson.

"I'm glad for your sake, Mr. Denahee. Still, I ain't staying."

Clarkson cleared his throat. "If you'll excuse us, I'd like to talk with Mr. Slocum in private."

Mrs. Baines waited till Denahee pulled her chair out for her and escorted her to the door. "Evan, come along." She summoned the boy, who was lingering, looking up at Slocum worshipfully. "Donal, I'll never be able to handle him. You tell him to come. He listens to you."

After the three had left, Clarkson turned to Slocum. "What's this about an Indian attack?" He sounded eager for a campaign.

"There was no attack. My guess is that someone dressed up like an Indian and scared everyone away, as well as doing some real harm to that geologist Schmidt. A service that was greatly appreciated, mind you."

"Not an Indian, huh?" Clarkson was still puzzled. "You know we've been having a lot of trouble with them Nez Percé. They're being very uncooperative. Some of them have attacked miners in other parts of the territory."

"Well, I can't say about those other incidents, but if it was an Indian, I think our Indian was perty well provoked. McBean murdered five of them, after all."

Clarkson shook his head. "That doesn't justify what they—or he—did to McBean."

"You got the story wrong, Clarkson. I did what was done to McBean."

"You scalped him?"

"McBean was scalped?"

"Ho, ho. You ain't heard yet." The marshal shivered and grinned. "McBean was scalped, and his head was severed from his body and stuck on top that pole by the mine."

"A grisly town, this Snake Gulch is. Now you see why I don't want to stay." Slocum paused for a moment, imagining McBean's scalped head at the top of the mine pole. "What about the body?" he asked.

"That was left where you shot him, I reckon."

"You find any pouches in his pockets? Any gold with my name written on it?"

"Sorry." Clarkson put on his hat. "He get all your booty?"

"I've got enough. Will have to get me a horse to get back to Lewiston, though. McBean and that geologist pushed that blue-roan of yours over the falls."

Clarkson shook his head as they left Duncan's. "I hate a man who pushes a horse over a falls," he said. "I'm not gonna stop you if you requisition someone else's horse. You've killed enough men, so I hear, to have a good selection to pick from."

Clarkson gathered his men together, and Slocum rode off, on McBean's black stallion, to Mamie's.

She was in her kitchen, busy as when Slocum had first seen her. "There'll be a big supper tonight," she explained. "Celebrating Mr. Denahee's return and things getting back to normal."

"Mamie, you'll be a rich woman someday."

"I'm planning on becoming a philanthropist when I get old." She laughed gaily and pulled him out the back door. "You're leaving now?"

Slocum nodded.

"Well, you don't have to look so relieved. I'll miss you. Really I will." She kissed him gently on the lips. He could have let the kiss develop further, but the men were waiting for him. "I've got something for you," she whispered.

Slocum let her lead him to one of the sheds. She lifted the bar and led him inside. The flint-eyed Ghost Horse stood in front of him, his nostrils flaring. Swung over his back were Slocum's saddlebags.

"So you're the Indian." He wasn't surprised.

"I am, actually. My grandfather was Witkispu, from Alpawa Creek. The same area Matthew came from."

"Why, I'll be damned. So you were listening to the coyotes."

Mamie shrugged mysteriously.

Slocum led the Ghost Horse out front and tied McBean's stallion behind him. The Ghost Horse wouldn't attack the black stallion that way. It was time to think about stud farming. He checked his saddlebags and found two pouches of gold.

"I took some of the bags McBean gave those boarders," Mamie confessed. "I killed my share of them, too, and they wrecked my house."

Slocum kissed her good-bye. A nice long, juicy kiss for all the neighbors to talk about for years to come.

As he followed the cavalry out of town, Evan Baines ran after him. "Don't go, Slocum. Don't go," he cried. "Slocum, don't leave me here. I want to join the cavalry, too!"

The boy was too young, though he'd matured some. "Take care of your mama," Slocum called back, and added to himself, "and your gold mine."

A special offer for people who enjoy reading the best Westerns published today.

WESTERNS!

NO OBLIGATION

Mail the coupon below

To start your subscription and receive 2 FREE WESTERNS, fill out the coupon below and mail it today. We'll send your first shipment which includes 2 FREE BOOKS as soon as we receive it.